The Day
the Sea
Rolled Back

Illustrated by Maroto

The Day the Sea Rolled Back

Mickey Spillane

 Windmill Books and E. P. Dutton

Library of Congress Cataloging in Publication Data

Spillane, Frank Morrison
The day the sea rolled back
SUMMARY: A man and his 12-year-old son lose all hope of
finding a sunken treasure in the Caribbean.
Then one day a strange thing happens to the sea.
1. Buried treasure—Fiction.   2. Caribbean area—
Fiction   I. Title
PZ7.S462Day   Fic   78-7855
ISBN: 0-525-61589-X

Published simultaneously in Canada by
Clarke, Irwin & Company, Limited, Toronto and Vancouver

Designed by The Etheredges
Printed in U.S.A.   First Edition
10 9 8 7 6 5 4 3 2 1

The Day
the Sea
Rolled Back

1

From the top of the eastern crest of Peolle Island, Vincent Damar watched the noon sun bounce magically off the gentle waves of the Caribbean. Until now, it had always been a sight to fill him with pleasure. The uncanny brilliance of the clear green waters that had such a delicious salty smell when the spray hung in the breeze made him feel a touch of sadness for all those city-bound people he had left fourteen years before.

But now the pleasure was only partially there. It had been four months since the *Blue Tuna* had plunged to the bottom someplace out there in that vast sea, an-

1

other victim of the sudden vicious line squalls that could rise unpredictably out of a clear sky and destroy anything not big enough to fight back.

Or was there something to the myth of the "Atlantic Triangle" whose southern corner enveloped this very area?

He let out an annoyed grunt and dismissed the idea. He had been on the side of science too long to pay attention to superstitions. It was science that had led him to this island in the first place, diverting his mind from his wife's death when Larry was born. In his research on the Spanish Plate Fleet of 1732, he had come across a remarkable document that pinpointed the sinking of the treasure-laden galleon *San Simon* somewhere off the reef that encompassed Peolle and Ara islands.

For a moment he grimaced sadly. Somewhere, in the ocean, could cover an awful lot of territory, he thought.

But he had sold the house on Long Island, picked up the 42-foot ex-Navy cutter, had it outfitted for salvage work, then took his son to the sparsely peopled atoll named Peolle and set out to astound the world of historical discovery with his new find.

Vincent shook his head in disgust. If he had been a fisherman, everything would have been fine. By now, he would have had a dozen friends scattered throughout the islands. But hint that you had a lead on a sunken treasure ship everyone knew was somewhere in the area, and gold-fever greed turned them into enemies who hated with a fierce anger.

For 140 years small clusters of coral-encrusted gold and silver coins had been washed ashore at various points, and nets had snared other isolated artifacts that definitely established the graveyard of that ancient ship to be somewhere between where Vincent was standing and the horizon thirty miles away. Unfortunately, the radius of that sweep made a gigantic semicircle that included several hundred square miles.

He still couldn't figure how it had happened. His boat should have been more than enough to weather that squall. The engine was running smoothly, they had been sailing into the teeth of the wind with no difficulty, rolling somewhat but not dangerously, enjoying the adventure, then . . . the *Blue Tuna* just sank. It just plain sank as if something had taken a bite out of the bottom, and he and Larry were in the dingy with the storm all around them and rode it out for eight hours before the weather lifted. It was another two hours' row to Ara Island and even before he had tied to the dock, Vincent knew there wouldn't be any real sympathy handed out to them at all.

Oh, they'd fake it, all right. Old lady Betts at the grocery would click her tongue, and Jake Skiddo, who ran the pumps, would give that wink that could mean anything, but they'd have that secret look of enjoyment like everybody else on Ara because the treasure was still out there where they still had a chance at it.

Crazy, Vincent thought. If they had it, what would they do with it? Not a doggone one of them would ever leave the place they lived in now. They'd only take it and bury it someplace else, then spend the rest of their lives guarding it, and when they died it would still be a lost treasure.

The Jimson brothers had been the worst, though. They didn't even bother to disguise their gloating. Bud Jimson had been standing on the dock and had said, "You city fellers oughta know better than to put that green water to the test. Joie and me, we barely got back ourselves and we been sailing these waters nearly forty years."

A surge of anger turned Vincent's face red. Most of his life had been centered around boats off Long Island, but he didn't say anything. Instead, he looked at Bud Jimson with eyes that had gone hard and curious. He was remembering the swirling cloud masses that had broken for a moment, just long enough so that he was sure he had seen the dirt-splotched hull of the Jimson boat on the same heading he was on. "Yeah," Vincent said, "I know. I tried to raise you on the radio when we were going down."

Bud Jimson glowered at him. "We never heard any call," he said abruptly. "Anyway, why would you call me?"

"Because you were running a couple hundred yards off our starboard."

There was no way of telling whether Jimson's expression was real or feigned. "Impossible! We were . . ."

"Forget it," Vincent said.

He had wanted to get back to Peolle right away,

but no one on Ara seemed to have any means of getting him there, even for hire. All the boats were lashed to the rickety dock, but according to their owners, all were in such need of repair that it would be days before they could be moved.

It didn't take long for the message to get through. The Jimson brothers had passed the word and nobody had the guts to buck them. They just lied, made excuses and cast anxious glances to where Bud and Joie were stowing gear away on the *Petrel*. Vincent and Larry were going to be stuck here on Ara until the mail boat came by in three days and the next stop after that would be Miami. By the time they got back to Peolle, the house they had built, their possessions, everything . . . would be gone.

He had been about to call it quits right then, but a voice with a strangely accented lilt called up from under the dock and said, "I say, Mr. Vincent, sar . . ."

The man was a Carib his own age he didn't recognize, but he remembered seeing his handmade sailing skiff out at sea many times. "Yes . . . hello."

"I'm Tim . . . short for Timothy, sar. From the backside of Peolle. If you don't mind riding with me, I'll be happy to take you back to the island."

"Mind?" Before another word was spoken, both Vincent and Larry were in the skiff, watching Timothy shake out the single sail. When they rounded the dock, Vincent nodded toward the Jimson brothers, who were watching them from the stern of their boat. "I think you just made some enemies, Tim."

From his spot at the rudder, Tim flashed a toothy grin. "Oh, no, sar. You have to hate to be an enemy. I do not hate them. My people were here before they came and they will be here after they go. They are just mean. I leave them alone. The sea will take care of them."

Vincent snapped himself out of his thoughts and looked down at the beach below where Larry and Tim's son, Josh, were crabbing. He whistled and, when they looked up, pointed toward the house. Larry waved back and indicated with outstretched fingers that they'd be there in five minutes.

Vincent took one last look eastward, wondering idly how such a clear green sea could conceal anything as large as the *Blue Tuna* . . . or, for that matter, the old *Nantucket Belle* herself.

And the *Belle* was what he had to explain to Larry before he left with Tim in the skiff to intercept the trade packet on its monthly run back to the Florida coast. Not that he expected any accidents, but in case one should occur, the secret of the *Nantucket Belle* would be in good hands, at least. Larry might be only a young boy, but the wisdom of maturity was already beginning to show.

When they had finished lunch, Tim and Josh went down to the cove with the stores for the skiff and Vincent unlocked the plastic fishing-tackle box on the table.

For a moment he hesitated and frowned. Larry

7

gave him a funny grin and said, "Pop, will you quit worrying about leaving us here alone."

"Come on, you're still my little kid." Vincent laughed.

"When do I get to be your big kid?"

"Maybe when you're ninety. That sound okay?"

Larry's eyes laughed back. "Sure is tough to be somebody's kid."

"Pipe down or I'll send you back to school on the mainland."

"I'm piped, I'm piped. I'd rather have you for my teacher. Now, what's with the tackle box? You said you were going to the bank, not out fishing."

Vincent reached in and took out a folded yellow document encased in a transparent plastic envelope. He laid it down carefully, then put a typewritten sheet beside it.

Larry was plainly puzzled. "What is it, Pop?"

"It's a page from the log of the *Nantucket Belle*, sunk in these waters in 1872. She was an iron-hulled, paddle-wheeled, three-masted bark whose master was another student of the Spanish raids on the gold coming out of the mints of Mexico City and Vera Cruz."

An expression of recognition touched Larry's face. "You mean . . ."

"The *Belle* located the *San Simon* and recovered most of the treasure. The Spanish wreck was in thirty-one feet of water, perfectly visible as a wreck at that time even though most of the wood had been destroyed by teredo worms. They anchored over the spot, and

8

teams working out of a diving bell removed what proved to be about ninety-five percent of her cargo of gold bullion and precious gems destined for the courts at Madrid and the church at Rome."

Larry finally nodded. "You know something, Pop?"

"What?"

"Now I know why everybody thought you were a bit nutty. The only natural place for one of those galleons to get hung up on the coral would be the extension of the reef off Ara Island. You weren't looking around anywhere near there."

"Oh, but that's where the *San Simon* is, all right. Her captain clearly marked his position in his log and it's still in the archives in Madrid."

"Then how come nobody can find it?" Larry asked.

"Let's see if you can remember some of the history I taught you," his father said. "What year did the *San Simon* set sail back to Spain?"

"1732," Larry told him.

"When was the first Toledon earthquake reported?"

Larry thought a moment, then: "Ummm . . . 1740. Two merchant ships in the area that managed to survive brought the news back."

"You remember what was special about that earthquake?"

Larry shrugged. "Just that there was a new island formed . . . and part of Oomlo fell into the sea." He thought for a moment; then understanding came into his eyes. "The wreck was still there, but the checkpoints the captain sighted in on had changed."

"Exactly. And the master of the *Nantucket Belle* finally figured it out."

The story fascinated Larry and it showed in the subdued excitement on his face. "But . . . the *Belle* . . . Did a storm get her too?"

His father shook his head. "No, it wasn't necessary. Gold fever and a mutiny did it all instead. During the on-board battle the boilers blew and the *Belle* went down like a stone. The First Mate had one single sighting before he went over the side with the logbook, and that one reference point he indicated was our cliff on Peolle Island, right here."

Larry's face reflected his disappointment. "Just that *one* point?"

"Apparently that's all he had time for."

"But . . . you can't triangulate a position from only one point."

Vincent ruffled his son's hair. "I know. Why do you think we were carrying on that pattern search for all this time?"

"Pop . . ."

"Yes, son?"

"If all the other islanders thought you were on a wild goose chase, why would they get all upset about what you were doing?"

"Good question," Vincent said. "My guess is that

somebody got on board the *Blue Tuna* one of the times we were getting supplies at Ara. They could have seen the copy I made of the page from the *Belle*'s log. They never got a chance to read it all or make a copy, but they knew I had information they didn't have."

"And if you looked long and hard enough, you'd find the wreck."

"Unless somebody beat me to it." Vincent paused, then slipped the papers back in the tackle box. "You hang on to this. Keep it someplace safe and don't let anybody near it. If anything happens to me, at least you'll have a crack at all that money someday. There is a critical distance factor in that log that will give you a headstart over anybody else."

"Come on, Pop, what's going to happen to you? Besides, who needs all that money?"

"Right now we could use a little bit of it. If I can't negotiate a loan, there won't be another boat, the property here goes back to the government, we go back to the mainland, where I'll probably teach school again and you'll be delivering papers for spending money."

"Really that bad, Pop?"

His father let out a small laugh. "Well, let's say you won't have to deliver papers."

"Pop . . . I hope you get it. I know you like it here . . . about as much as I do."

"I know, son. Just don't sweat it. Something will turn up. It always does." He grinned at Larry's seriousness. "At least we've got something going for us."

11

"What's that?"

"Both of us like fish," he said.

"And sleeping on the sand under a tree isn't too bad either," Larry added.

"Until it storms," his father reminded him.

2 The day after his father left, Larry and Josh
netted their day's haul of fish just before
noon. They picked out an eight-pound snapper for their
supper, kept a pair of conchs aside to be dropped in the
tidal pool by the house for a later meal and emptied the
net back into the sea. Having fish die on the beach for
no purpose at all didn't make sense to either of them.

When they were cleaning the net, Larry looked up
and spotted the boat a half-mile offshore. Josh followed
his glance and said, "That is *Petrel,* the boat of the
brothers Jimson."

"I wonder what he's doing around here."

13

"Well, he is not fishing, there is nothing to salvage out there, so I imagine he is looking over this place to see if anyone is at home."

A momentary glint of the sun bounced from the stern of the boat. "He's got glasses on us," Larry said.

"Then he sees us, so he will not come in."

"He'd better not!"

"What would you do, Larry, if he did?"

"Come on, Josh, you know what I'd do. I'd get you on the bicycle mount to grind the generator, get the power up and call the Coast Guard on the emergency channel."

"But the Coast Guard station is a long way off."

"Not by helicopter, it isn't," Larry told him.

"Well, I don't think you'll have to call. Look."

Offshore, the *Petrel* was making a 180-degree turn and when she was headed north again, she gradually faded into the distance.

Josh was grinning as he rolled up the net. "See, you scared him off."

"Yeah, sure," Larry chuckled. He threw the loops over the end of the net to secure the roll, then glanced up at the sky. "What time do you think it is, Josh?"

"Maybe about one o'clock, eh?"

Larry made a wry face. "I didn't think we were here long, but look at that sky."

"Funny color."

It was peculiar. A yellow-orange haze that didn't seem to come from anywhere and gave everything a faint pinkish glow.

14

"Think it's a storm coming in?"

Josh raised his head, sniffing the air with eyes half closed. It was something that only the Caribs seemed to master and they were never wrong. "No . . . there is no storm."

A gentle breeze touched the back of Larry's neck, coming out of the east. For some reason goose bumps raised the bleached hairs on his forearms. "You feel that?"

Josh nodded. "The wind shouldn't be from that quarter."

"I don't like it," Larry said. "Let's see what's on the marine radio. If any freak storm is headed this way, we'd better be ready for it."

But there was no storm warning on any of the channels. The weather reports from both marine and aviation centers were for warm and clear days through the next week at least.

Outside, the yellowish look deepened and the wind dropped a few degrees in temperature. But there was no unusual wave action at sea and the birds flew until just before sunset. Larry and Josh ate their supper, figured the strange atmospheric condition was probably due to an off-course dust storm from the mainland, then hung their hammocks from the trees outside the house and went to sleep.

There was no logical explanation for what had happened during the night. No scientist saw it, no sophisticated machines recorded it, no great populated areas were affected by it.

It just happened.

And it was seen.

Larry and Josh could very well have been the first to see it.

Sometime during the night the sea had rolled back and left the bottom a great barren place splotched with giant coral heads, stretches of dark purple vegetation and strange rolling configurations that still glistened wetly in the early light of dawn.

The smell was different, too. The normal salt tang was sharper now, enhanced with a wet, weedy aroma from the vast acres of marine growth that were lying flat against their sandy beds. Above it all, even now, the boys' senses could detect that minute organic smell of dead things that hadn't escaped and had already begun decaying in the first sunlight.

The awe of the incredible sight sent a chill up their backs, and Josh's voice was almost inaudible. "Larry . . . what happened?"

"I don't know."

"The sea . . . the water—it isn't there any more."

"Whatever it is . . . we saw it coming last night. Remember the odd color in the sky . . . and the wind from the wrong direction?"

Josh nodded. "You think . . . it could be . . . well, a tide, a very low tide?"

"If it is, this one goes all the way to the horizon." Larry turned, squinting toward the north. He could see

the very tip of uninhabited Ramu Island, and although there didn't seem to be any water there either, there was no way of determining just how far the condition extended.

"Larry . . . what would your father, with all his schooling, say at a time like this?"

For a small moment Larry suddenly felt as though he were fifty years old. Then he shrugged and said, "Well, what goes up has to come down, so what goes out has to come back sooner or later."

"Your father is a very smart man."

"That's what I *think* he'd say," Larry explained.

Josh was grinning, a glint in his eye. "Would he say . . . that such a time should not be wasted?"

Now Larry was feeling a tug of adventure. The initial uneasiness couldn't last long with youth and he knew he was smiling at his friend. "Is that what *your* father would say, Josh?"

"That's what my father would say, even though he is not a man of much education."

"We'll never get another chance, will we?"

"I don't think so."

"Then," Larry said, "let's go see what the sea has left behind."

They ran to the beach, slowing as they neared the point that formerly had been the low watermark, then stepped out gently, testing the consistency of the sea floor. It didn't take them long to discover that it wasn't much softer than the surface behind them. Some areas were sandy, others of more solid coquina, and where the sea grass grew, it was simply spongy but firm. Within fifteen minutes they were able to choose the sections that gave the best footing and stay away from those that were still wet enough for them to sink down to their knees.

Three hundred yards out they came to a spot they both knew well, the fluke of an old, rusted anchor from some ancient ship. A wide growth of weed almost covered it, running in a long S pattern between four huge coral heads. Until now it had been a favorite fishing place, and the holes that housed the groupers that lived there were gaping wide open, still wet but empty of occupants.

"Everything's gone," Larry said. "You see anything?"

"Just some crabs buried in the sand back there. No fish except one dead one."

They stood there a minute, surveying the emptiness around them. Finally Josh said, "Are you thinking the same thing I am?"

"About how far to go out?"

"Yes. And how quickly we can get back if the sea decides to return."

Larry chewed on his lip a moment, giving thought to the situation, trying to recall all the many details he had scoured from books in his father's library. "You know, Josh . . . the sea leaving like that . . . it was a quiet thing, like a continual tidal flow, so it's probable that it will come back the same way. At any rate, if we keep a close eye on the horizon, we'll see an immediate

19

reflection when there's any change. That ought to give us plenty of time to get back to dry land."

"Or we swim a lot," Josh put in. "By the way, what are we going to do out there?"

"Look for an old iron wreck. It was called the *Nantucket Belle.*"

Six miles north two nervous men were trying to recover from the shock of finding themselves anchored to dry sand an hour's run from their dock. Joie Jimson's face was white with fear of the unexplained, and as superstitious as he was, his voice was still stuck in his chest. Bud was tougher. He had no idea of what had happened either. They had anchored offshore for the night, hammocks swung from hooks in the stern. They never felt the water leave or the boat settle crookedly on the bottom, because the hammocks kept them in a stable position. Now he was sore at Joie for shaking like a scared old woman just when certain new possibilities were opened to them by the good graces of nature.

He still had to admit to himself that looking at what had been the bottom of the sea was an unnerving experience. It wasn't as he had imagined at all. There were hills and valleys that weren't at all discernible from the surface, depressions that could conceal the wreck of a boat or even the remains of a ship from anyone standing on the sea's floor.

Overhead the birds were collecting but, instead of diving, were settling onto the wet sand to snatch live, wriggling things from their seabed nests. Bud Jimson had dived enough on these bottoms to know the consistency of the sand, so he had no qualms about going over the side to test the solidity of his footing.

Joie finally found his voice and said, "Doggone it, Bud, you crazy?"

"Knock it off, will you. I know what I'm doing."

"Doing? The only thing to do is to get us outa here!"

"Think you can do it better up there on deck?"

Joie took a startled look around him and licked his lips.

"Now, go get the fire ax and get yourself down here."

"What do ya want the ax for?"

"To make you ask stupid questions, dummy. Just do what I told you."

When Joie had tossed the ax down, it took all his nerve to clamber over the tilted railing and slide down the side of the hull to the sand. He was clumsy about it and the barnacles ripped his pants and carved a few furrows into his hide.

Bud watched him with disgust. "Why didn't you come down the other side?"

Joie shrugged, looking foolish. "I dunno."

"Look for a boat."

"What boat?"

"The *Blue Tuna,* that's the boat!"

"But it sunk . . ."

For a moment Bud Jimson was about to lay his

21

heavy hand right across his brother's jaw, but that wouldn't have made him any smarter either. "I know it's sunk, but do you want everybody to know *why* it's sunk? You think we're the only ones that'll be out there. Come on. Just as soon as they get their nerve up, everybody from the island will be scavenging for anything they can find."

"Yeah, but there's no fish . . ."

"Oh, you nitwit," Bud said. "The wrecks, the wrecks! You know how many wrecks are around here that we never knew about?"

It finally dawned on Joie what his brother was speaking about and a tight greedy look edged into his grin and he nodded quickly.

Bud looked back toward Ara, then checked the sun's position overhead. He pointed in a southeasterly direction and said, "This way, come on. And don't step in any of those soft places."

Had they a mind to, Larry and Josh could have made a fortune saving the lead sinkers they yanked out of the sand by their leader lines. So far on their trail they had left four fishing poles with reels too corroded to be useful any more, two cheap watches and a 35-horsepower motor that had been underwater a year or so. They had skirted a dozen wet sinkholes they knew would be like quicksand, then had come to a flat, moist depression that stretched a hundred yards on either side of their course.

Josh said, "What do you think?"

"Let's try it slowly. I'll go ahead and you be ready to grab me if it gets soft."

"Okay."

Treading gently, the boys eased forward. Larry was concerned with the area immediately about his feet and didn't look up until he heard a loud hiss behind him. He stopped suddenly and turned around. "What is it?"

Josh was staring straight ahead, his finger coming up to point at the sand. "Look."

Larry followed the direction of the finger, then involuntarily took a step backward, his breath catching in his throat. Very gradually, a huge section of the sand in front of them was rising, an area as big as a tractor trailer heaving upward until suddenly there was a gap in the sand as something brown and horny with great scale-markings barely began to show. Only inches of it were visible for a 30-foot length, but it was hemispherically shaped with a serrated ridge running lengthways down its middle.

Without realizing it, both boys were holding each other tightly. Until now, this walk on the seabed had been a fun thing, but now stark reality was facing them. "You know what that looks like, Josh?"

Softly, Josh said, "Almost like the back of a turtle. They do that in the ponds on the island."

"If that's a turtle, and we're only seeing part of him, do you know how big it is?"

"We will know better when he lifts his head up. Then we will see."

They looked at each other, startled. "Then he will see us, too," Larry told him.

"I would not like to be here then."

"Maybe it's not a turtle," Larry suggested.

"A *something else* would be even worse. Let's not wait to find out," Josh said.

In their haste to get away from the area, they nearly stumbled and fell several times, but when they reached the solid bottom again they turned and stared back at the great wet depression. Whatever had risen out of it had gone back again and it seemed like just another placid spot at the bottom where the sea used to be.

"Who would believe us if we told them?" Josh asked. "I can hardly believe it even though I saw it." He paused for a moment, thinking, then, how there were strange beasts out here, huge beasts they saw only after the great hurricanes. Sometimes they would attack the boats and once they destroyed a village above the beach. "I always thought they were just silly stories to scare children."

"Now you know," Larry said.

"I liked it better when I thought it was just a story."

Larry's face squinted in a frown again. "My dad always said there's no way of telling what's at the bottom of the sea. Things there never have any reason to come up and it's only by accident we ever get to suspect their existence at all."

This time Josh's tone was very somber. "Larry . . . we should be very careful, no?"

"Very careful . . . yes," Larry said. "In fact, the

25

next time I'm fishing and something awfully heavy that shouldn't be in these waters hits my line, I think I'll cut loose instead of trying to reel it in." He nodded toward the northern end of the wet spot and they headed that way, angling around it, then taking the gradual dip down, pointing toward the rise that seemed to spread over several acres, covered with the dark purplish weed that was beginning to emit an odd odor from standing bared to the sunlight.

It wasn't until they had reached the edge of the mound that Josh put his hand on Larry's arm. "Look," he said, separating the grasses. "Ballast rock!"

A few yards farther on they got a better look at it. The rock ran up the slope a good fifty feet and even some of the worn and eaten timbers were visible protruding from stones. Whatever ship it had been had ground itself to destruction on this abrupt peak in the sea's floor.

Larry pulled several of the rocks out of the pile and studied them. Each one weighed about fifteen pounds, rough, angle-edged rocks with tops layered with coral encrustments. He tried a few more, then nodded. "A British ship, most likely. They used any old rocks for ballast. The Spanish were a little more particular. They didn't want to cut their hands passing these things on board, so they selected only smooth stones."

"Pirate vessel?"

"Merchantman, most likely. There would have been a pile of cannon around if it were a pirate ship."

"Wouldn't merchant ships carry guns?"

"Not if they could help it . . . or could get protection from the fleet. The more guns, the less cargo, and they were out for trade goods. If we looked, we'd probably find a few small brass cannon, the anchor and some old relics."

"Would it be worth poking around later?"

"I doubt it," Larry said. "The only good thing would be those brass cannon and they're probably under tons of sand." He looked back, checking his position from Peolle Island. "We're a mile and a half offshore now. Let's see if we can make it to Skittle's Rocks."

"But Skittles is another mile out. I thought we were . . ."

"We were over Skittle's when the *Blue Tuna* went down," Larry told him. "Someplace in the same area was the *Nantucket Belle.*"

They choose to climb over the slope of the ridge rather than take the long way around in the softer sand. They scrabbled for footholds in the irregular crevasses of the ballast rock, then got past them and hauled themselves to the top by grabbing hold of the thumb-thick sea grasses. When they reached the peak they squatted there and caught their breath, searching the vast dry area in front of them.

It was a distinct vantage point, that was sure. For the first time they were able to make out shapes that from the water's surface had meant nothing. A quarter-mile away was Pierre Combolt's old two-masted hulk that had been torn from the dock at Ara last year and

27

had been thought disappeared forever. Now here it was, upside down on the bottom, the green paint of the hull blending perfectly with the grasses around it, dotted with clusters of barnacles that disguised it. From above, it was unidentifiable; from a side angle view, it was evident what it was, even down to the pair of broken masts that jutted out to the side.

"How would it turn over like that?" Josh asked.

"Dad said hurricane waves in waters this shallow can do almost anything. Once that wreck got set in the sand, it was there to stay."

Josh nodded and swept his arm out in an arc in front of him. "Do you see that trench there?"

Larry saw it, all right. He followed the line of it with his eyes, a mile-long gap in the ocean bed that ended in a large circular area on either end. "It looks like a long, skinny dumbbell."

"It's filled with water," Josh said.

"I don't remember that being there. We've sailed over that area plenty of times and our depth finders never showed it."

"You know," Josh said, "it could be like the rain. When the water runs off downhill it makes new channels and new holes. Maybe when the sea went back the water running around these hills dug itself that trench."

"Well, we can always swim it . . . and we'd better not wait too long. A few more hours and we'll have to turn back."

Carefully, they picked their approach path to the gorge in the sand, staying on the lanes that gave them the most solid footing. Behind them their footprints were blazing a natural path for them to follow on their return, which made them feel a little easier about what they were doing.

When they reached the edge of the channel they stood back from the soft, sloping sand and saw it for what it was. "You were right, Josh. This whole section is soft as mush, and the water carved out it's own skinny lake. If it hadn't happened, we never would have known how to cross it. The place must have been like quicksand."

"The banks still look pretty soft," Josh said.

"Well, we can dive in from this side and scramble up over there. I'm a little bigger than you, so supposing I go first, then give you a hand up on the other side."

"Fine," Josh told him. "You better get a good run to hit the water. Looks like it's not very deep."

Larry couldn't back off very far. He planned his dive, took three fast steps forward nd pushed off and hit the water in a shallow belly flopper. A few strokes took him across and he dug into the sand with his hands and knees, clawing hard to get to a place that would support him. When he made it, he turned around and waved to Josh. "Your turn . . . let's go!"

Josh grinned and followed Larry's lead. He hit the surface and splashed his way across, laughing at the experience.

But Larry wasn't laughing. He was yelling at the top of his voice for Josh to hurry, his face pinched with terror. He had caught the movement out of the corner of

29

his eye just in time . . . the two dull gray angular triangles sweeping around the gentle bend of the sea's new canal, the dorsal fin and tail of a shark that was reacting to the splashings in the water and was putting on a sudden burst of speed to reach his prey before he could escape. Josh had lived on the edge of the sea all his life. He recognized the urgency in Larry's voice and his laugh froze in his throat and he put everything he had into the last few strokes and the last time he turned his head for a breath of air he saw the surging of the water from the back of the monstrous fish that came at him like a missile. He saw the tail make a final sweep, the mouth open, but Larry had him by the arm and with that wild strength given to people in moments of life and death emergencies, Larry snatched him up the sand and they rolled onto the top together.

For a few minutes they couldn't move. Their hearts were still pounding furiously and when they finally calmed down, Josh said, "That was a tiger shark."

"I know." Larry nodded.

"How big, you think?"

"Too big. He could have swallowed both of us."

"Why would he be there, Larry?"

"Who knows what a shark is going to do? I imagine he found that trench when the water was going out and got himself stuck there. Nothing else seems to be moving in that water, so he just keeps cruising around. We must have sounded like a good lunch to him."

"That was close," Josh said. "The shark, he can move very fast."

"I wouldn't want to go through that again," Larry said.

He got a strange look from his friend. "We may have to," Josh reminded him. "We have to go back."

3 The Jimson brothers were competent seamen, but in this new environment they were
totally out of place. So far they had covered a half-mile
from their grounded boat, but they were wet and sandy
from numerous falls into the sinkholes and had just
begun to select the better isles of travel from hard experience.

"I hope you know what you're doing," Joie said.

"Shut up and save your breath." Bud looked at his
pocket compass a moment, snapped it shut and put it
back in his pocket. "We're not far from Skittle's Rocks
now . . . maybe an hour."

Joie heaved a deep breath and looked behind him. Ara Island was a dim smudge on the horizon. But between them and the island there were a few dots of motion that hadn't been there before. "We'd better get moving then. Company's behind us."

Bud said something under his breath, his face dark with annoyance. "Everybody and his brother is gonna be out here treasure hunting today."

"So why do we have to mess around with the *Blue Tuna?* Okay, so you don't want anybody to know how it sunk . . ."

Holding back his anger and explaining as if his brother were a child, Bud said, "Everybody's looking for the *San Simon,* right?"

Joie thought a moment, then nodded.

"Now, Vincent Damar, he never bothered looking where everybody thought the *Simon* went down, did he?"

"Nope . . . that's why we thought he was dumb."

"He was smarter than everybody, you blockhead. He studied up on that wreck. He found out that somebody else salvaged it first and that the salvage boat got sunk too. It's probably around Skittle's Rocks, because that's where Vincent Damar was doing all his searching."

"Then let's go there and forget about the *Blue Tuna,*" Joie whined.

"Oh, you flounder head. If anybody reaches the *Tuna* and finds that tank in there with our name on it, we'll be looking out from behind bars for the next ten years. You had to be dumb enough to use one of our own tanks to sink somebody else's boat. Brother!"

"Come on, Bud. Who knew this was gonna happen? It was just supposed to sink and that was the end of it."

"Ever hear of diving gear, stupid? Suppose the wreck was located and they decided to use SCUBA and look it over."

"Yeah, I guess you're right, Bud."

"Okay. Now pick up that fire ax and let's go."

They stepped down from the mound carefully, their feet wetly slapping the sand. The bottom was changing now. The sand was darker, the grass in smaller clumps and the gradual drop-off very discernible. Both of them knew that had the sea been in, they would have been fifty feet below the surface. Even though they were dry now, it was an unnerving thought. What made it worse was that they had no direct line of sight ahead, the curves of the bottom leaving only a small area visible in front of them. The worst part was, they didn't know when there might be a sudden inrush of the sea itself. It had gone out quickly and quietly. If it returned the same way, it could sweep them right along with it. Bud considered all of this but didn't want to mention it to his brother. He was afraid Joie might panic if he realized the possible consequences.

Overhead, the sun was a bright, burning disc making heat waves rise from all directions. As the sand heated and the water evaporated, a haze of wispy steam seemed to hang over the bottom like a gentle ground

35

fog on land. All around their feet small things trapped in a warming sand bed began heaving themselves toward a cool environment, making the bottom crawl as though it were alive. Joie made a disgusted sound in his throat and closed the distance between himself and his brother.

Directly before them was another of those strange-shaped hills, larger on the east side, falling off sharply, and it wasn't until they got around it that Bud held out his hand and stopped abruptly. There, jutting out of the sand, were huge, water-rotted timber stubs aligned in such order that they both knew they were looking at the partial skeleton of a centuries-old wreck. Ten feet farther on, the confirmation was complete. A great chain lay coiled in the rock-strewn rubble, almost hidden by the grass and coral, that ended at a mighty anchor nearly buried under the debris.

Both the Jimson brothers could read the ballast rocks. It was a Spanish ship, all right, but whether or not it was a gold-laden galleon, one of the plate ships carrying silver, or an empty vessel enroute to the Mexican coast, they couldn't tell. The pair of cannon visible on the side of the mound wasn't indicative of anything either, but the sight of them made Joie's hands shake with anticipation.

"Bud . . . ya know what we got here? We got ourselves a wreck . . . a real Spanish wreck. It ain't even on the charts. Nobody even knew about it before!"

"We're not looking for that," Bud yelled at him.

"Maybe you ain't, but if you think . . ." Joie took

36

a swing with the fire ax at a lump of coral and powdered it into a shower of pieces that came apart and left a lump of pure tar standing black against the sand.

Bud forced himself to be patient. He took out his compass, climbed up on the wreck and managed to find Ara in the distance. He scribbled on a pad, then took another fix on Ramu Island, which was still visible, estimating the distances, noting the directions and writing them all down. "What're you supposed to be doing?" Joie hollered up at him.

"Making it easy for us to find the place when we come back, stupid."

"It's easy now! What are we gonna do when the water's back?"

With total exasperation, Bud said, "Dive, you nut. We're the only ones who know it's here. Right now we haven't got time to waste. Later we'll have plenty. Now, do you savvy that or do you want me to draw you a picture?"

Joie grunted and shrugged. "Guess you must think I'm pretty dumb, huh, Bud?"

"Now why would I think that?" Bud said. He took another look at the wreck that had lain there hidden for so many years. No wonder you could sail over them for a lifetime without ever knowing they were there. It was only by sheer luck that they were ever uncovered at all. They might have gone down a mile away, and following storms could have rolled the hulks this far in. If they did, treasure could be scattered all over the seabed. But at least they had a starting place. Bud patted the paper in his pocket. As long as he had the map, he thought, this wreck was only the beginning.

Larry and Josh stood at the base of "The Old Lady," the largest of the nine natural rock outcroppings that thrust themselves up from the sea floor to take the bottoms out of countless hulls whose navigators never knew they were there. All around the sand were parts of both wooden and iron ships that had lost the battle of survival to those jagged peaks . . . planks with rusted spikes, yard-square pieces of torn iron plating, chunks of machinery and parts of rotted cargo.

The peaks of Skittle's Rocks were just high enough to tear the guts out of a ship like a deadly knife wound, letting her live long enough to clear the rocks and die a mile or more away. Larry remembered his father studying a chart one night, speculating on how far a ship could last after an impalement, sketching in a rough circle he intended investigating when his present project was completed.

And right now Larry could appreciate the possibilities in this quest for gold. How many millions of dollars in bullion from the bowels of Mexico was scattered over the area within view from the cliff at Peolle Island? The archives at Madrid, Spain, told one story of the immense treasure, but the other—that of what was being stolen by the ship's captains and crew and not accounted for—was another. His father had told him it could have been as much as half again the listed amount.

Larry was silent a long moment, deep in thought. If they could only stumble over one single bar of bullion, or a congealed mass of silver coins, the kind in McKee's museum . . . his father wouldn't have to beg the banks for a loan or mortgage his future at all. They could renew the lease on their part of the island, they could get another boat . . . all they had to do was find the tiniest fraction of the wealth strewn so close to their own home.

Josh snapped him out of it when he said, "From the top of the rock you could see everything, Larry. There is no higher point."

"Yeah, you're right. Let's try it."

"Be careful of the coral. A cut from it can give a bad infection."

"Right, Josh. You want to take the side on my left?"

"Let's go," Josh said.

They climbed slowly and carefully, picking their hand- and footholds deliberately. Twice Larry paused, to work rusted pieces of metal and a foot-long iron spike out of the coral that covered them, mementoes of deathly kisses between nature and man in years past. Beside him, Josh was reaching for the final plateau and when they both heaved themselves up on the crown of "The Old Lady," they knew they were doing something no one had done before.

Now their visibility was almost unrestricted. They could see the ever increasing angular drop-off of the bottom that dipped another fifty feet a quarter-mile away before leveling. They knew that another mile out the great drop began that went down to the immense depths where strange creatures lived in total darkness.

But where was the sea? The heat waves and drifting fog obscured nearly everything past the quarter-mile range, and there was no telling what was happening out beyond. Josh had his hand shading his eyes, peering into the north, staring at something intently. After a minute he said, "Larry . . . whose boat was just painted a very bright red?"

"Why . . . that's the Jimsons'."

"Look." He pointed so that Larry could follow his direction. "Just a small spot of red, right near the horizon. See it?"

Larry nodded. "Yeah, yeah. I see what you mean. But it could be something on the bottom . . ."

"Not that color red," Josh interrupted. "It's still new and shiny. See the way the sun bounces from it."

"They must be stranded out there."

Josh shook his head. "Wait." He shaded his eyes again, cutting out as much glare as he could. Then he realized what had bothered him. There was a pair of dark dots out there, slowly moving in their direction. "Look, they're not stranded. They're coming this way."

After a moment Larry spotted them too. They stayed in sight a full minute, then a rise of sand cut them from view. "Let's get down," he said.

"What do you think they're after?"

"The same thing we are," Larry told him.

Together they turned and started back down the way they had come, but then something stopped Larry. For a brief instant he was able to see between the Skittle's Rocks and what he saw made his hands clutch the coral tightly.

"What is it?" Josh asked.

"I think . . . I spotted the *Blue Tuna*," Larry told him.

"You sure?"

"I couldn't miss the shape of that hull. It hasn't been down long enough to break up and is lying there just as nice as you please."

"How long will it take to get there?" Josh asked.

"About fifteen minutes, I'd say."

"Well, if those *are* the Jimson brothers over there, it'll take them at least an hour to reach here . . . which should give us enough time to do what you think we have to."

Without another word, they finished their climb to the bottom, then, using the sun as a guide, headed for where Larry saw the wreck of their boat. From the rock it didn't seem like a difficult trip at all, but once again, the "terrain" was a series of depressions and weird hillocks they had to circumnavigate to reach their destination.

They rounded what they thought was their last outcropping of coral and thought they'd be on the flat, but what had appeared that way from a position above, wasn't that way at all. It was a long, conical ridge that

41

tapered to slim ends, completely sand-covered with narrow paths of grass running over it to subvert its shape completely.

Both boys gave a shrug of annoyance and trudged alongside the ridge, staying away from the yard-wide rivulet of water that still bordered it. They were on the shady side and there was activity in that still water. There were some creatures that didn't go out when the sea left and twice they saw the glint of eyes and the slow movement of teeth-lined mouths and pulsating gills.

A coral bulge protruded from the center of the mound and Larry picked up an empty conch shell and threw it at the protuberance. It connected with a dull smash and the pieces scattered across the bottom.

But there was more than that. A crack appeared in the coral, widened and, with a sharp snap, split away from the rest of the mass and smashed itself against the sand below.

There was wide-eyed wonder in their faces when they saw the metal that was beneath the coral. There was another muted crack and a huge slab simply slid off like melting snow from a rooftop. Josh gasped, "Larry . . . !"

And Larry knew what it was. He would have been able to tell from the shape of the mound and the center projection if he had studied it carefully, but with the coral falling off of its own weight, exposing the unmistakable structure beneath, there was no doubt at all.

"That's a submarine," he said.

"A . . . submarine?"

"What you're looking at is a conning tower. The sub's lying rolled over on its side."

"But Larry . . . there is no submarine here. My father, he would know about these things. He was here all during the war . . ."

"Not that war," Larry told him.

"What do you mean?"

"Look at the length of it. It's only a little thing compared to the newer subs. And look at the thickness of that coral growth." He paused for a moment, edged up to the exposed metal and ran his eyes across the surface. Along the rim of metal he saw a stamping. He couldn't read it, but the language was identifiable. "That's a World War I German submarine, Josh."

"Here?"

"Oh, it's not impossible. Others have been discovered in pretty shallow waters before."

"How could they get in here, Larry? This is no place for a . . . a submarine! Why . . ."

Larry interrupted him. "They didn't intend to come here. Don't forget, that war was a long time ago and the machinery was almost primitive. You know what a Kingston valve is?"

Josh shook his head.

"Well, it's a valve that lets the water come in to submerge the boat and lets compressed air blow the water out so the sub can surface. Sometimes those valves got stuck when the boat was underwater, and that was the end of the journey for the crew. It might have taken months, or even years, but when the air leaked past the Kingston valve, the boat almost floated again and tide and wave action washed it ashore . . . or at least into these waters."

"And . . . you think . . . there are still . . . people in there?"

"Long dead if they are."

"Larry, listen to me . . ."

"Come on, Josh, we're not going to go in there. In the first place, we can't."

Josh looked suspicious. "What's the second place?"

A serious look crossed Larry's face. He realized the importance of what was here and the place it could take in history. "My father could report a find like this and I bet the government would be glad to help recover the boat."

"But isn't it . . . well, sort of like a big coffin?"

Larry gave it a moment's thought. "True, but look what they did with the *Arizona* at Pearl Harbor. In a way, this is a memorial too, and it is a piece of history. Anyway, I'll let Dad decide."

Josh nodded and glanced at the area around them. "You know, Larry, I'm not scared. *Really* scared, I mean, but I'll sure be glad to get back on the real beach."

"That makes two of us, but we have things to do first." They walked to the end of the tapered ridge and from the partially covered bulge they knew they were at

44

the stern. Under that smaller mound would be the single propeller and rudder.

"Think we can find her again, Josh?"

"Sure. It's right in line with the last two peaks of Skittle's Rocks. Maybe six hundred yards off. It'll be easy to find now that some of the coral's off that place."

"The conning tower," Larry told him.

Josh took another look at the strange shape. From where he stood the outline was clear and he felt a cold chill when his mind tried to picture the interior of that steel casket. He turned around, glanced past Larry, then said softly, "There's the *Tuna,* my friend."

Bud and Joie Jimson hadn't elected to go around the obstacles they came across. Somehow, they seemed to think they could make better time with a straight course, but it didn't take them long to find out how exhausting it was to scramble up damp, sandy hills, the grit filling their shoes and scraping away at the skin of their feet. Both of them had coral scratches on their arms, and the spines from a sea urchin had pierced Joie's canvas shoes and gouged holes in his heel. Walking on the toes of one foot was wearing him down fast.

They lay on the crest of a sand pile, the stink of the drying seaweed coming up around them now, and Joie said, "Man, let's stay here awhile. I can't go much farther."

"You'd better, little brother, or I'll leave you here alone."

45

Joie licked his dry lips and swallowed hard. "You wouldn't!"

"Try me and find out. Right now I'm so sick of your complaining I could feed you to the crabs."

"Bud . . ."

"Knock it off." He turned over and lay on his stomach. "You look where I'm pointing, Joie, and maybe you'll see something."

"Where?"

"Follow my finger, dummy."

"You mean that dark thing way over there?"

"That dark thing's the *Blue Tuna.*" He frowned, annoyed. "Can't you ever tell one boat from another? Look, the hull lines. You can still see the mast and there's not a speck of weed on her yet. She hasn't even been down long enough to collect a barnacle, but if anybody gets to her ahead of us, you know what we'll collect."

Joie didn't bother glowering back at his brother. He simply shrugged and said, "Then you better move a little faster, Bud."

"What're ya talkin' about?"

With a nod in the direction of the *Blue Tuna,* Joie said, "There're a couple more dark things out there and they move like people."

Bud felt the sand grate between his teeth and he yanked his brother to his feet and gave him a shove down the other side of the hillock. He even jerked the fire ax from his hand to be sure it wouldn't be dropped

46

and his fingers were wrapped around the handle as if he wanted to smash something with it.

Right then Joie was sorry he had said a word. In Bud's mad anger they'd both be pushed at a killing pace across the treacherous sand and he was already practically exhausted.

4 It was an eerie feeling, walking around the boat like this. The *Blue Tuna* was lying on its port side, her pennant still attached to the masthead. Almost as if she were sleeping, Larry thought. The fishing rods were still in their brackets, and chrome and brass fittings still had a sheen to them under the sun, although the salt had begun it's destructive work on most of her.

He walked around the stern, his hand touching the transom lovingly, then dropping to the big brass propeller. He leaned on it, felt it move slightly, but even now corrosion was making inroads against the fine metal.

Josh had gone toward the bow and was waiting for him beside the gaping hole in the bottom of the hull when he got there. Larry looked at the gap in the wooden planking. He and Josh could have gone through that opening at the same time. Whatever had done that had delivered a death blow so quickly it had almost engulfed the crew.

He reached up and felt the edges of the exposed planks. There was something about their color and shape that annoyed him. They weren't jagged or fresh-looking around the rim, but black and smooth, and when his fingers touched them, pieces crumbled into his palm. The wood was pulpy soft for a good six inches back from the edges, almost as if it had been eaten and digested.

"It looks like it was burned," Josh suggested.

"That's no burn," Larry said. "What could burn it?"

"Spilled gas in the bilge, a spark . . ."

"Gasoline would float on *top* of the bilge water."

"Did you *have* any bilge water?"

Larry shook his head. "Very little. The *Tuna* was a pretty dry boat and Dad kept her in good condition. Besides, if it had been a fire, we would have had a whiff of smoke. There was none of that."

"Ah," Josh pointed out, "but you were in a storm. The hatches were closed; the wind was in your faces."

"No, we would have had some indication. All we knew was *wham* . . . and the bottom fell out. Suddenly

49

we were knee deep in water and going over the side." He nodded at the hole. "You know how many gallons of water could come in there in ten seconds."

"I don't like to think about it," Josh said.

"Me either, but I sure want to know why it happened."

"You're going in, aren't you?"

"This isn't an old sub."

"Okay." Josh grinned. "I'll go in with you."

They went back to the port side, hoisted themselves in, reaching for handholds to help them up the inclined deck. It was still damp, coated with a slimy natural carpet of sea algae. Gradually, they inched their way to the mahogany doors that led below and with a sharp kick, Larry broke the small brass lock and the doors flew inward.

Light streamed through the starboard portholes, gleaming off the water that still filled the hull like a half-emptied cereal bowl. Another larger shaft of light came in through the uneven hole in the bottom, splashing over the engines that were still crusted with grease. A pair of life jackets bobbed on the surface, surrounded by unopened coffee cans, part of a wooden catwalk and his dad's floatable tackle box.

Beneath Larry's feet, three steel bottles of compressed air were wedged under the steps and he kicked them loose, watching them roll in the oil-slicked water. He moved gently, working his way closer to the gap in the bottom. There was something peculiar about that hole and it took him a full minute to figure it out. The thing extended from the raised keel up between the ribs and stopped on an almost even horizontal line. But when he looked at the sides of the ribs and keel around the hole, they had the same charred effect too.

No, it wasn't an outside force that had ripped the boat apart, and it certainly wasn't a fire. He knew *what* had done it, but didn't quite know *how*.

Until he looked at those compressed-air bottles floating in front of him. They used to be in a rack on the side and when he felt for it his fingers pulled out a metal strap that had been cut almost all the way through before the surging of the storm had broken it loose. Then he saw the other bottle . . . or what almost looked like a compressed-air bottle. It was six inches in diameter and two feet long; but it was painted green, the top that he knew had never been tightened down was gone and there was a glass liner inside the steel.

The only thing that bottle ever held was a deadly corrosive acid, and when it fell, its contents hit the bottom and began eating its way outside through the boat. It wouldn't have taken long to rot through the planking; then one hard thrust from the sea would finish the job and engulf the *Blue Tuna* before anything could be done about it.

There was a grim smile on Larry's face. He had seen bottles like that before. They were nested in forms outside the Jimson brothers' boathouse.

He grabbed the metal bottle and pulled it out. Then

51

he heard Josh call him and his tone was urgent. He hauled himself back to the doors, edged through to the deck, his feet braced. "What is it?"

"There . . . see? Two of them. They're coming this way."

Larry squinted against the sun, nodding. "That's Bud and Joie, all right."

"What're we going to do, Larry?"

"Not stay here, that's for sure. We're only a couple of kids and they're not going to let us tell what we know." Josh gave him a sharp glance and Larry explained what he had found. To Josh, the death of a boat was a serious thing, and when it had been deliberately caused, with no concern for those on board . . . He could feel a terrible anger fill his chest.

"For once, Larry, I wish I were grown up. I wish my father and yours could be here to meet them. I wish . . ."

"Wishing isn't getting us out of here," Larry said. "Look, let's go over the other side and keep the *Tuna* between us and them. If we head in any other direction right now they can cut us off, but if we get far enough away we can get lost behind the grass or one of those sand hills."

"You forgetting about our footprints?"

"We have to take that chance. If we're lucky the damp sand will fill them in. Let's go."

Keeping low, they scrambled up the slippery deck, then flipped over the side and let themselves down to the sand. They took off at a slow run, knowing they had to conserve their energy. Any pounding gait would drive their feet so deep in the sand they'd tire quickly, besides leaving behind an indelible path to their location.

Whenever they slowed they'd check back to make sure they were positioned properly, the *Blue Tuna* their shield from the Jimson brothers, but they knew they didn't have too long before they would be spotted. Their only hope was to cut down the incline toward the great drop-off where the seabed was darker and they could merge into its shadows. There they would be safe from the Jimsons. But if the sea came back . . .

Bud Jimson almost ran the last hundred yards to the *Blue Tuna,* his eyes on the other set of prints that were still evident in the sand. Joie was beside him, panting for breath, his eyes bulging from the exertion, but his brother was almost elated. He wasn't thinking of Larry and Josh as two boys . . . no, to him they were the *enemy* and enemies had to be destroyed before they destroyed you. He gripped the ax tightly and stopped, his fingers holding Joie back.

"Quiet now. They're inside. We have them."

"Bud . . ."

Without answering him, Bud pulled himself over the port railing. He looked at the shattered hatch doors and grinned, a mean twist to his lips. He knew what he was going to do and he wasn't worried about it at all, because when the sea *did* come back, it would dissolve all evidence and the boys' disappearance would simply

53

be listed as another tragedy that happens to curious islanders.

But something was wrong. If they *were* in there he could hear them and there was no sound at all, absolutely nothing coming from the interior of the boat. He slammed the edge of the ax into the deck, grabbed the edge of the cowl and hauled himself toward the door. He said something nasty under his voice, then scrambled inside. It took only a minute to locate the tank and another to find the top. When he got back outside he grabbed the ax again, tossed the tank and the ax over the side and jumped down himself.

Joie had already found the footprints on the other side. He showed them to his brother, staying well out of the reach of his hand. When Bud got mad he'd take it out on him and he wasn't in the mood to get splatted again.

This time, though, Bud wasn't all that mad. He had gotten what he had come for and planned to bury it somewhere away from the boat. That would take care of that. Then he could follow those doggone kids and take care of *them*. Right now, they could be standing between him and the dream of a lifetime.

Joie was dumb but not *that* dumb. He knew what his brother was planning and he was feeling sharp pangs of nervousness eating into his chest again. He grabbed hold of Bud's shirt before he could move off and stopped him. "Look, Bud, why you want to chase them kids now for? Gee, they get their fathers on us and we're in big trouble."

55

It was time he told Joie, Bud thought. Joie wasn't much for bravery, but he was a greedy slob, wanting everything the easy way, and if he knew what the deal *really* was, Bud wouldn't have any trouble with him at all.

He made the decision, turned and looked at Joie with a cold, hard stare. "Do you think Vincent Damar went back to the mainland without telling his kid everything about the old salvage boat that located the *San Simon*'s treasure?"

"You mean . . . that little kid knows . . . ?"

"That kid's a smart one and don't you forget it. His old man's got special permission to teach him and already he knows more than kids what go to the island schools. Right now those kids are after that wreck and if they find it first, we kiss it good-bye. All I know is that it's an iron wreck, a three-master about a hundred years old. I never got a chance to read everything Damar wrote down, but I got that much. Now, do you want us to have that new boat and the big times on the mainland with all the money we can spend or do you want them kids to do us out of it?"

Bud had called it right. His brother was seeing that big picture of city lights in his mind and the greed was clenched in his squinty eyes. "We're wasting time," Joie said, and when he started trotting beside the rapidly fading footprints he wasn't even limping any more.

Something seemed to have happened to the light. The sun was still there, moving slowly in a great arc across the heavens, but the odd texture of the bottom absorbed all the reflective qualities and Larry and Josh had the strange feeling of being on another planet.

The temperature had changed, too. Even the heat had gone out of the sun and there was a cold, clammy feel to the air, one that clung to the skin like an early winter's wind, a reminder that things wild and terrible were to follow.

They had gone into the dankness of the incline hoping to pick up a southerly path that would take them parallel to the great drop-off, then cut back to the west around the undulating hills of sand to stay out of sight of the Jimsons, but so far no solid path had showed itself.

Josh was to the right of Larry, peering around anxiously. Ahead was ever a deeper gloom than where they were, and the wet spots were getting more frequent. Somehow, the sun wasn't evaporating the water in this area at all. When he pointed this out, Larry said, "Most likely there's more water under the sand. If the sea were in, we'd be sixty feet beneath it right now."

"It's getting awfully soft, Larry."

"Yeah, I know." He paused and let his eyes drift toward the sky. "I wonder what time it is."

Josh followed his glance, peering through the unnatural gray haze that filtered out the usual sharp glare of the sun. He wasn't at all sure of the angle of the bottom he was standing on and couldn't position the sun the way he could on land, so he shook his head ruefully and said, "The morning has gone passed, Larry. Right

57

now we are at the halfway mark . . . the . . . How do you say it?"

"Point of no return?" Larry supplied.

Josh nodded, his face solemn. "From here we go back . . . if we want to get back before dark . . . or before the tide comes in."

Larry pointed toward the northwest. "Then let's take the upslope around the side of that coral ridge there. At least that will keep between the Jimsons and us for a little while." He turned and checked the tracks they had made a few minutes ago. "Although at the rate the sand is filling in," he said, "they're going to have to be awfully lucky to trail us."

"Larry . . ."

"Yeah?"

"Suppose they catch us."

A grimace passed over Larry's face. He didn't like to think about it at all.

"Would they . . . ?"

"You know them as well as I do, Josh," Larry told him.

"Then we'd better hurry."

But out of sight, some distance away, Bud Jimson had anticipated their next move. He held out his hand to slow his brother down and said, "We'll lose those tracks if we go down into the drop-off."

"So what'll we do?"

"They have to come up. Sooner or later they have to head east again or the sea'll get 'em."

"Why don't we just leave 'em here and . . ."

58

"Because they know that as well as we do, stupid. Would you like to go wandering down in the big drop?"

"No . . . no, sir, Bud. I don't want any part of that."

"They don't either. Now, what we got to do is reach them or cut them off. I don't care who gets 'em, us or the sea, just as long as they are *got,* understand?"

"Sure, Bud."

"And as far as the law is concerned, the sea got 'em and who's to prove different?"

Joie nodded. "I hope we got enough time," he said.

"We have," Bud told him.

5

But time was one thing that Larry's father had run out of. Vincent Damar left the office of the Lissop bank in Miami and headed toward Biscayne Boulevard. The Lissop people had been the third and last of his financial contacts and when they turned down his request for a loan, he realized that it was all over.

What he really dreaded was having to tell Larry. His son's faith in his ability to solve any impossible problem was so great he was afraid that news of their being utterly wiped out would be a terrible shock to the boy. It might not have been so bad if he hadn't had that solid gut feeing that they were closing in on the wreck that held all their hopes. Until the *Blue Tuna* went down, he could actually feel the nearness of that old hulk as if his body were a magnet, picking up emanations from that old steel hull.

However, feelings weren't the things you could borrow money on. All that was left in the account was barely enough to get themselves and their limited possessions back to the mainland with enough left over to last about two weeks while he found himself a job.

Vincent Damar looked at his watch and frowned. As long as he was here in Miami he might as well use his time as best he could. For a month or two he could take any job that would keep the two of them secure while he re-established his teaching contacts for something more permanent. They were going to need a place to stay, nothing expensive, and close to a school for Larry's benefit.

When Vincent had decided on his program for the rest of the day, he bought a newspaper to scan the job ads and see what was being offered in cheap housing. Luckily, it was off-season and something might be available right away.

He didn't realize how deep he was in his own thoughts until a couple of kids on bicycles almost ran him down. He started to yell after them, then stopped. For a moment he just stood there, wondering what had gotten into everybody. Not one person was coming to-

61

ward him. Everyone was headed toward the water. The newsboy was closing his shop and Vincent said, "What's happening around here?"

"Got me, mister," the boy said. "They're all saying something's happening at the ocean."

"Now, what can happen to that?" Vincent asked in exasperation. "It's a beautiful day."

"Who knows? Maybe a whale got beached. Why don't you go see?"

There *was* something exciting about the way everyone was all worked up. There didn't seem to be any indication of a disaster—no whistles were blowing or sirens screaming and the police cars that went by were at normal speed. It was just that everybody else was hurrying and anxious to get down to the beach. Then suddenly Vincent grinned, tucked the newspaper under his arm and followed the crowd to see what it was all about.

Twenty minutes later Vincent *knew*.

Around him the crowd packed together as if looking for mutual protection, their voices almost stilled. No one needed to ask what had happened; it was right there in front of them, so big and broad any explanation would be impossible.

Inexplicably, the sea had pulled back a full half-mile, laying bare the footings of that great city. Boats were tilted at crazy angles on the sand; ropes that had held them tied to docks snapped like threads. Shell-crusted pilings of the piers looked like giant insect legs all standing in silly puddles of salt water.

Except for the few boat owners trying to salvage their craft, nobody was yet venturing near the wet sand. The mild surf was twinkling out there as the gentle waves broke and receded, all as calm and serene as the lull in the eye of a hurricane.

Vincent glanced upward and scanned the sky. A good dozen airplanes were skirting the area and he recognized their military silhouettes. At least the Air Force had gotten on this sudden quirk of nature in a hurry. A pair of helicopters were cruising the shoreline and television cameras were recording the phenomenon for the evening's news.

The activity seemed to start at the southern end of the beach. The solid front of the crowd softened, then broke, clusters of people getting over the startling sight and succumbing to their curiosity. Vincent saw them starting toward the vast emptiness, beginning to walk out onto the mushy bottom.

Unlike the others, Vincent worked his way back to the street. It was all too evident to him that the people regarded this as some local freak condition. They had seen unusual tidal action before, and wild situations where the ocean had gone berserk, and to them this was just some new oddity to add to their collection.

But Vincent was thinking scientifically and he was worried. He was faimilar with oceanography and was positive this wasn't a simple local event. The ocean was a giant that didn't do things in little ways. Whatever had

63

happened had to have had a start, and the origin of this oceanic display would probably be miles to the south.

And that's where Larry was!

Vincent looked at his watch and knew he'd have to hurry. The street and pedestrian traffic had thickened, all headed toward the water. He picked his way around them, cut west a block to where it was less crowded, and half-ran until he came to the Andra Radio Shop. A year ago he had purchased his marine and base radio from Bill Andra and knew he had good working equipment in his shop.

Luck was with Vincent. Bill was just about to close down and go see what all the shouting was about, but Vincent waved him back inside the store and told him what he had seen. Then he added: "Look, around here it's a curiosity. Everyone seems to think it's simply local, but who can tell what's happening in other places?"

"But nothing's been on TV yet," Bill told him.

"There hasn't been time."

"If the tide's out that far . . ."

"Look, it could go back pretty far before anyone would think anything about it, and the slope of the bottom is shallow enough to let it happen pretty fast."

Bill nodded sagely. "What can you do about it?"

"Let's see if we can raise Larry on the radio. That far south, the situation can be totally different."

"Okay." Bill nodded toward the transmitter on the desk. "You try to get him. I'll see what I can pick up on Air Force and Naval frequencies. And you might as well turn on the local radio channel on my portable over there. Some news might be filtering through now."

Ten minutes later they were both looking at each other across the room, strange expressions on their faces. The local radio had played up the incident as if it were part of a Chamber of Commerce promotion for a new show . . . and how the public was enjoying the new view from an old ocean front. One thing the newscaster did mention, however, was that the tidal effect was felt north as far as Fort Lauderdale, where it seemed to fade out. Dozens of explanations were given for the occurrence, but no two were the same.

Vincent said, "Anything from government sources?"

Bill shook his head. "Negative. There are a lot of military planes being scrambled but all for observation purposes. One thing is funny, though."

"What's that?"

"An awful lot of code is suddenly going out. Nothing I can make sense of. How about Larry?"

"No response. I tried a few others I know but can't raise them either."

"There's *got* to be radio traffic on those frequencies, Vinnie."

"Sure, and everybody is trying to talk at once. It's so scrambled you can't make sense of anything."

From the stricken look on Vincent's face, Bill knew what he was thinking. "Any way you can fly back?" he asked softly.

There was a somber note in Vincent's voice. "Only by seaplane, and under these conditions, I doubt any pilot would take the chance. If there are any choppers available, you can bet they'll all be chartered by photographers by now."

"It'll have to be by boat then."

"Any boats around here are all grounded on the sand." Vincent's hands knotted into fists with helplessness. "I'm stuck here, Bill."

"Look," Bill said, "Larry's a smart kid. He's not alone down there. If anything's happened, there will be a lot of people to help him out."

"Yeah," Vincent told him, "that's what I'm afraid of." For a moment his mind had envisioned an expanded picture of what had happened in Miami and he realized that the reaction of the island natives would be completely different from that of the city-bred people of this area. The world to the people of the islands was the water and any drastic change in it would provoke unusual reactions.

Bill watched him a moment, then suggested, "Why don't you try monitoring those marine channels until something comes through? If this thing has touched your area the base stations should be working overtime."

"Maybe not, Bill. Very little of the heavy marine shipping comes close to the islands. The small boats that do know the area so well they go on radio traffic."

"Won't hurt to try. At least it'll keep you busy."

Vincent nodded in agreegment and sat down at the receiver. He fitted the headset over his ears, flipped the power switch to on, then began a routine search of the airwaves.

Five hundred and twenty miles to the southeast, the freighter *Emory Welsch* rolled slowly in the mild swells of the Atlantic. It had been an easy crossing from the African coast and the weather forecast had looked good for another two days. Captain Stephen Morelli relaxed on the bridge, anticipating their arrival in Jacksonville, Florida, and three quiet weeks at home, away from the vast emptiness of the ocean.

Not that he didn't enjoy a gentle passage. The only trouble was, a quiet trip was just too boring. He welcomed a storm at sea and even small mechanical difficulties—anything to break the monotony. Unlike the other officers and the crew, he had no hobbies to occupy his time, and the languid days had seemed to drag by.

For the past two hours he had been staring out the sturdy window of the bridge, his mind far away from the sea itself. But then something seemed to tug at the innermost reaches of his thoughts, trying hard to attract his attention, and he frowned lightly, letting his mind come back to the present.

What was it trying to tell him? He gave a momentary start as he glanced outside a moment, then looked down at his watch. To be sure, he checked the position of the sun and the frown deepened. He looked across the maze of instruments to where his first mate was checking a chart. "Doug . . ."

"Yes, Captain?"

"Come over here and take a look at the ocean."

The mate laid a heavy metal ruler and his dividers on top of the chart and walked over to the window.

From the expression on his face he seemed to be viewing something for the first time too. Like the Captain, he peered up at the sun, then scanned the horizon. "Strange color, sir."

"What does it look like to you?"

"Like sunset, but we're far from that time."

"Ever see it before?"

"Only when we were under a very heavy dust cloud. There was that time off Aden . . ."

The Captain interrupted him. "But there's no dust in the air at all. Now take a good look at the water. Since there's no dust and the sky is clear, it couldn't be an atmospheric reflection, could it?"

After a minute of deep study, Doug shook his head. "If I didn't know better," he said, "I'd think we were seeing the bottom . . . deep down, but a bright, sandy bottom." He glanced at Captain Morelli quickly, turned and went back to his chart. When his tracing finger found what he sought, he nodded and rejoined the Captain. "According to the chart, we should have twenty-two fathoms under us."

"Let's be sure," the Captain said somberly. He went to a side panel, switched on the Fathometer and watched the pattern of the ocean's bottom register on the screen. He checked the depth, and the frown on his face deepened.

Something had happened to six fathoms of water! If the charts were correct and their own position properly estimated, something had dropped the surface of the ocean thirty-six feet closer to the bottom!

"Mr. Andrews . . ."

Doug swung around, startled by the sudden formal use of his last name. "Yes, sir?"

"I'd like verification reports from any ships in the area. Contact the Coast Guard to see if any change has been noticed in this section or if any error could possibly have been made in depth soundings."

"Yes, sir."

"And bring back somebody to stand by the Fathometer every minute. I want to be informed of every change." When Doug hurried off to the radio room the Captain turned to the helmsman. "Ring for half-speed and hold a steady course."

"Aye, sir." The helmsman's hand shifted the position of the engine room telegraph and almost immediately the noticeable throb of the *Emory Welsch*'s single propeller eased as the RPM's decreased.

Captain Stephen Morelli was feeling better again. Finally, some excitement had come into this drab ocean-crossing and a new spirit of challenge was surging through him. It might all be a false alarm, a simple error in printing on the charts, but at least it was something to think about.

Ten minutes later Doug Andrews was back with a seaman, whom he stationed at the Fathometer before he went up to Captain Morelli. His face was grave as he handed over a typewritten report. "From the Coast Guard, sir. They want position and depth reports every half-hour."

"They've suggested a course change," the Captain noted.

"Apparently as a result of signals from other ships

69

closer to the mainland. All vessels west of us have been ordered farther out to sea. From what I could learn, there has been a severe tidal drop along the southern part of the Eastern Seaboard."

Captain Morelli pushed his cap back and took another look at the ocean, as if he were seeing it for the first time. "Impossible!"

"I'm sorry, sir. I even intercepted signals from the Mexican coast. Nothing exceptional has happened there yet, but they were making inquiries. We even picked up a few panic calls from independent stations on the mainland who are tying to find out what's happening."

"Did the Coast Guard advise on the weather situation?"

"Not yet, sir. We've already notified those who asked what the condition was here, so they're alerted."

"What about emergency calls?"

"Nothing. So far all ships seem to be safe. The Jacksonville port is still open, but Miami is diverting all ships to other areas."

"Very well. We'll make this course change and head for Jacksonville. We can always stand offshore if necessary."

"Yes, sir."

"And Doug . . . please stand by the radio personally. I want all information brought to me immediately."

In Miami, Vincent Damar slipped the headset off and leaned back wearily. Since he had come in, the back room of Bill Andra's shop had become more like a noisy bus station. Everybody was looking for information not available on the streets or from commercial sets and it took a good hour to get the crowd out and the doors locked.

Bill threw up his hands in a gesture of disgust. "With all the brains they're supposed to have in government, you'd think just one of 'em would have an answer to all this."

"It's never happened before."

"Let's hope it doesn't happen again. What did you pick up?"

Vincent shook his head. "I spoke to an officer on the *Emory Welsch*. They're in water shallower than it's supposed to be, so the condition is going out to sea."

"Any others?"

"Two more. They all reported the same thing."

"What were their positions?"

"All southeast of the Florida coast. Whatever it is, it doesn't seem to have any effect much north of here." He paused for a minute, his face taut. "I've got to get back some way, Bill."

"I wish I could suggest how," his friend said. "I just spoke to all the marinas in the area. Nothing's open and any boats out in the ocean are staying there. The Coast Guard is even planning a refueling run to keep anybody out there gassed up." He waited a moment, studying Vincent's expression, then said, "You did try *all* the islands, didn't you?"

Instead of answering, Vincent simply nodded.

"They wouldn't leave their radios, would they?"

Vincent let out a sour grunt. "You don't know that bunch, Bill. To them, the situation isn't a tragedy at all. It will be one big, grand opportunity to salvage anything that ever touched the ocean's bottom and they'll tear anybody apart who gets in their way."

"But . . . your kid isn't like that, is he?"

Vincent looked up slowly, his eyes meeting his friend's. "Bill . . . have you forgotten what a boy's curiosity is like? You think Larry could resist exploring an empty ocean bottom?"

"So let him, Vinnie. He's not going to get in anybody's way, is he?"

"Only if they figure out he knows more about a few things than they do."

It took a minute for it to sink in; then Bill realized what Vinnie was talking about. "Does he *really?*" Bill asked him seriously.

"I'm afraid he does," Vincent told him.

6 Jake Skiddo and Petey Betts had a sick feeling in their stomachs when old lady Betts told them the Jimson brothers were the only ones not safely accounted for. Every other boat was stranded beside the dock on the island, their owners accounted for and already out scrounging the great sea bottom for any booty they could find.

But the others didn't matter. It was the Jimson brothers who owed the most money to Jake and Petey, and if anything had happened to them, Jake and Petey would be out of business. It wasn't uncommon for the Jimsons to stay out overnight, but ordinarily they would have left word at the store. And to make it worse, there had been no radio contact at all.

Either the islanders had no imagination at all or they had too much of it, but they had gone to bed with the ocean in its usual place and awakened with the ocean almost gone, and how it had happened made their minds boggle. All Jake and Petey could picture was a giant outsurge of water sweeping all craft in front of it, making fish bait of any crews unlucky enough to be aboard.

Neither Jake nor Petey was adventurous enough to want to walk very far out onto that damp sand. Their lives had been spent by the sea and they knew what she could do and they didn't want to be in the way if and when she decided to return.

They were at their wits' end when old lady Betts got annoyed at their whining and told them they ought to get that crazy contraption of young Oliver Creighton's. She had seen him go through the swamp and across the beaches in the thing and since he was always out of money, a couple of dollars ought to rent it for a while. Jake and Petey didn't need any more urging. They ran for the pickup truck, hopped in and headed for the Creighton place before anybody else got the same idea.

What Oliver Creighton had was a homemade dune buggy. It wasn't much more than a VW chassis and engine with four outsize tires that not only would keep the rig going in soft sand but would actually float it if the need arose. It was ugly, but it was rugged and useful—

and it was Oliver's prized possession. Not only did Jake and Petey pay heavily for its use, but they guaranteed in writing that Oliver would get the pickup truck if the dune buggy was lost.

Heading toward the ocean, Petey said, "If we find them Jimsons, you can bet I'm putting everything this cost on their bill."

"You think they'll pay it?" Jake asked.

Petey grinned and nodded. "They got any choice?"

For a scant minute, Larry and Josh thought they'd be plucked from this wild situation they were in. The faint drone they had heard from the sky grew louder and both boys looked up, their eyes searching for the plane that made it.

"Coming closer," Larry said. "Hear it?"

Josh was peering at the deepening color of the sky; then he saw the speck in the northeast. "There it is!" He pointed excitedly, then began frantically waving his arms.

Larry followed the direction Josh's finger had indicated. The plane was there, all right, but much too far off for them to be seen by the pilot. It started to turn and for a moment their hopes faded, but when it turned back, sweeping in a wide arc, Larry said, "Bud and Joie Jimson won't want to be spotted, that's for sure."

"What do you mean?"

"They can't afford to let us get out of here."

"But . . . where can we go?" Josh asked. "If we go into the drop we'll never get back out. Look how wet it is already. There's no place left to hide!"

"We don't have to."

"Why not?"

"Because Joie and Bud will be doing the hiding. Right now I'll bet they're digging into the bottom like a couple of sand crabs to keep that plane from seeing them. If that's the case, then we can make a run for it."

"Larry . . . suppose they're still looking for us, though."

"That's the chance we have to take. You ready, Josh?"

"I'm as ready as I'm ever going to be." He looked at the plane that was getting larger as it neared their area. "Man," he said toward the plane, "just keep hanging around."

They couldn't really run. It was more like sloshing, like being in the middle of a bad dream with some wild monster chasing them. Their feet simply didn't want to move, sinking ankle deep into the muck before they came loose with a loud *slurp*. Their leg muscles tired, but they couldn't rest and their breath was like fire in their lungs.

Both of them fell twice but struggled up again and lurched toward the one small rise ahead. That monster behind them wasn't a dream—it was real and big and, right now, a deadly thing that wanted to leave them forever in the wet, salty sand far from the island they had left.

76

Overhead, the dull sound of the airplane was a comforting sound. It came closer each second, but the arc it turned in would keep it too far off for them to be seen. Larry turned his head once, slowing down for a quick look at where he thought the Jimson brothers would be. A pair of small dark areas could have been their forms, but the distance was too far to be sure. If the spots were the Jimsons, they weren't moving, just lying still with their heads down.

The boys looked at each other in silent recognition of the new problem facing them. The sand was firmer now, but to get to the protection of the sand hill, they had to cover a flat open distance the length of a football field, and if at any time during the run the Jimsons lifted their heads, the two boys would certainly be seen.

And that would be the end of them. With no trouble, the Jimsons could angle across and cut off any escape route toward the land. The boys were young and quick, but they were up against two strong men consumed with murderous hatred, a completely uneven match.

"Let's go," Larry said.

A brief rest had given them a second wind and they plodded ahead as fast as their feet could move. Behind them their tracks were in the drier sand but already filled in where they came up out of the drop. If the Jimsons thought they were still there and followed that path, the boys' chances of getting free grew better every minute. If they could only make the area where the bottom grew its mounds and hillocks and the weed lay between the

77

great coral heads, their size and agility would even their battle against the size and strength of the men.

They were almost there, breath coming in huge sobs that choked and burned, feet like lead weights dragging them down. Only a little bit farther . . . but in the sky the airplane had turned away, its drone getting weaker and weaker and Larry and Josh knew that now the Jimsons would be getting up and although the boys were close to the hill, they would be in plain view of the men.

Fingers clawed into the sand. They squirmed and rolled with a final effort, bodies so tortured with the pain of their exertion they couldn't even speak; then they were behind the mucky pile of sand that could well be made into their graveyard.

Behind them the Jimson brothers had risen to their feet. Bud was looking toward his left, a small scowl starting to appear between his eyes.

Jake Skiddo held the wheel of the dune buggy with all his strength while Petey was clutching at the upright of the rollover bar beside him. From the beach it looked like an easy drive across the open bottom of the ocean, but it was a deceptive vision and they were being tossed about worse than if they were in an open boat during a hurricane. The oversize wheels would sink in and drop them on one side, then just as abruptly carom off a half-hidden coral head and almost throw them loose. Unseen forces tore at the tires, wrenching the wheel in

Jake's hands, and he was beginning to wonder how long they could keep it up.

They weren't alone out there at all. It seemed as if the entire population of the island was probing every mound and hillock for anything they could use, finding long-lost anchors, wrenching brasswork off sunken hulks, edging ever seaward, alert for the one thing they knew was there and all hoped to find—the treasure ship.

One other thing everyone was doing—they were looking for the Jimson brothers. The island was much too small for anything to go unnoticed or for any rumor to be squelched. They all knew that the Jimsons were hiding something ever since Joie Jimson had bragged a little too much to Arnie Snyder, and if anyone had an indication of where that ancient trasure ship lay, it would be them.

Or Vincent Damar. The islanders couldn't understand it, but Damar didn't even bother to disguise what he was doing. Not that he talked openly about his project, but the planned courses he sailed in the *Blue Tuna* spoke for themselves. Vincent Damar was clearly searching for something on the bottom and the only thing of any value as far as the islanders were concerned was the wreck of the *San Simon.*

Since Joie Jimson had hinted that they knew of Vincent Damar's plans, the islanders kept a wary eye out for what Joie and Bud were up to. The Jimson boat was fast and the brothers unscrupulous, but the islanders had their own schemes as well and they watched both Damar and the Jimsons.

And now, with Vincent Damar in Miami, they had

to watch only the Jimsons . . . if they could find them. It wasn't until Jake and Petey showed in that weird contraption of Ollie Creighton's that they cursed their luck for not thinking of that dune buggy first. Most of them were already laden down with articles that were junk compared with what the *San Simon* carried, but they didn't want to give up their new finds any more than they wanted somebody else to beat them to the wreck. For the first time they were beginning to learn how painful the disease of greed could be.

Only the original natives of the islands escaped the ravages of the disease. Discovering treasure was something they had never been interested in. To them, whatever the sea took to itself, there it belonged. The fish, the conchs, the crabs—all these the sea gave up, but she kept the treasure for herself. So the old-time islanders sat back and laughed at the mad scramble for baubles so long ago consigned to the sea's bottom.

Laughter, though, was not part of Jake Skiddo and Petey. Their bodies were stiff and sore from the jolting ride, their stomachs as sick as if they had been to sea in a skiff. For the past hour they had crisscrossed the area, eyes alert to any sign of the Jimsons, when Petey finally said, "Let's hold it awhile, Jake . . . I can't take any more."

Neither could Jake, so he steered to the top of a weed-covered mound, the dune buggy vibrating over the strange, uneven surface. "Okay," he told his partner. "We need to gas up anyway. Grab that can out of the rack."

Wearily they poured the gas into the tank, emptying out their last drop. They both knew there was a limit on their exploration now. They could go just so far before the diminishing fuel supply demanded an immediate return to Ara Island. They both looked back at the buggy's tracks, noting the way water filled in the hollows in the sand. Any attempt to walk back from this point would end in disaster. The oversize balloon tires kept the dune buggy on the surface, but a man alone would go knee deep into the quagmirelike sand.

While they rested they squinted out at the vast empty bottom around them. There were moving dots of people on all sides and, strangely enough, their voices were carrying over that great wet plain.

"You think somebody will find the *San Simon?*" Pete asked.

"Ain't never gonna be a better time."

"They found other ships. How come the *Simon's* such a ghost?" Before Jake could answer, Petey added, "Maybe she's never even been."

Derisively, Jake said, "She's been, all right. Ain't they found the papers on her in Spain? And how about those cannon Reggie's pop dragged in?"

"Come on, Jake, that was fifty years ago and he never did remember where he got them."

"He just never found the spot again, that's all. But they were Spanish cannon and dated. The one in Miami even had the ship's name scratched into it."

Pete shrugged at that, still not convinced. "How about all the people who looked for that wreck so long? They shoulda found *something.*"

"Like what?" Jake countered. "The worms woulda eaten all the wood and the ballast rocks could get covered up. Even if there was cannon around, it would be so covered with coral you couldn't tell it from anything else." He eased himself off the dune buggy, stretched and said, "Like that stuff there, see?"

Jake pointed to a pile of coral at the bottom of the weedy hillock. Like most everything else, it was just a long, shapeless, coral-covered lump that smelled fishy now that it was exposed to the air. He stepped down the slope, tugged an open-end wrench out of his back pocket and gave the coral mound a whack. The whole side of it fell off.

Underneath was the pitted black cast-iron barrel of a cannon.

Jake couldn't get a word out.

Above him, Pete almost broke his leg clambering off the dune buggy.

Together, they stood there speechless, looking at each other, then back to the cannon again. Roughly, Pete grabbed the wrench from Jake and began hammering at the other sections of the coral, exposing more of the casting until there was no doubt at all about what they had discovered. Then the both of them attacked the other mounds. In fifteen minutes they had chipped away enough coral to realize they had nine separate cannon lying along one side of the mound.

Only then did it occur to them that the weed-covered hillock topped by the empty dune buggy was not just a plain sand hill at all. At close look, it had a definite size and shape. Without a word, they both scrambled to the top, took another good look, then began digging into the sand.

They didn't have to go far. No farther than a foot down they hit the first layer of large smooth rocks that could only be one thing. They were the ballast rocks of a Spanish ship.

Softly, almost in amazement, Jake said, "We found her. We found the *San Simon!*"

But Pete wasn't the quiet type at all. There was nothing important he could say in a whisper. He threw up two handfuls of sand, stood up with arms outstretched and shouted at the sky, *"We got the* San Simon!"

His voice traveled like all the other voices, and they all heard. And there he was standing, silhouetted perfectly for all to see, and when they dropped whatever they were doing and converged toward that sandy, weedy knoll, Jake was swinging at Pete for being so stupid as to give away the site of their treasure ship.

Had Bud Jimson studied that distant movement a moment longer he would have realized it could have been only Larry or Josh, but another bouncing movement caught his eye and he turned, squinting through the heat waves that bounced off the sand.

"What is it?" Joie asked, trying to find what Bud was watching.

"Somebody's got a vehicle over there."

"Can't no car go on that sand, Bud."

The look Bud gave his stupid brother made Joie pull away from him. "What's that thing then?"

Keeping one eye cautiously on his brother, Joie studied the strange contraption a few moments. "Well, guess it *could* be *some* kind of car."

"Jughead," Bud said. "It's that dune buggy Ollie Creighton put together. Nothing else could go out here."

"You think . . . they're looking for . . . the kids, Bud?"

"No way," Bud told him. "That buggy came from Ara, not Peolle. If anybody's looking for anything, they're looking for the *San Simon.*"

"What we oughta do . . . ," Joie started; then Bud gave him another fierce look.

"What we're gonna do is find those kids . . . Now, you hear?"

"Sure, Bud, sure. Let's go. All we got to do is follow their tracks."

Larry let out his breath with relief. He and Josh saw the Jimson brothers pick up their old trail and, for the first time in hours, they knew they might have a good chance of getting out of this enormous trap. Carefully they edged around the mound and, when they knew they were shielded from sight, took off at a fast pace, almost heading into a sun that was well on it's way past it's zenith.

85

The day had turned a more peculiar color of orange than before and the damp breeze had a chill to it that was completely out of season, but it was a comfort to the boys, who had worked up a sweat that dripped from their fingertips.

During a pause Larry noted the sun's position and estimated the time. His best reckoning gave them an hour's distance from the Jimsons . . . if the brothers had accepted the fact that they were still roaming along the lip of the coastal drop-off. As long as the boys could maintain that distance they were safe. Neither of the Jimsons had the stamina or the fleetness of youth, and each succeeding minute made the situation look better. In fact, Larry was already relishing the thought of telling his father what had happened. It wouldn't take *him* long to square things away with the crooks from Ara.

Larry's calculations would have been correct, too, if Petey Betts hadn't let out that joyful whoop when he and Jake Skiddo found the *San Simon*. The sound of his voice had rolled in an enormous wave across the barren ocean bottom, the peculiarities of nature amplifying and carrying it like a mirage all the way to where the Jimson brothers were standing.

"Bud . . . did you hear that?"

"I heard."

They were looking in a different direction now, at a 20-degree angle to the right of the sun. "Somebody found . . . the *San Simon*." Then Joie's eyes caught the wildly moving figure of Petey Betts on top of the mound, so far off that he was barely a speck. "There, Bud . . . see him!"

But Bud wasn't so concerned about that waving figure. He was looking at all the other dots starting their move toward the center of the action, and a slow grin started to play around his mouth.

"Let's go, Bud! We can't stand here and . . ."

Bud turned to answer his brother and by sheer accident his eyes picked up what appeared to be a pair of thin lines that circled around a dune an eighth of a mile away. He peered again, carefully, then nodded. Had the sun been overhead he never would have noticed those lines, but now, at an angle, shadows made them more apparent.

"Didn't you hear me, Bud? I said . . ."

"I heard what you said," Bud said bruskly.

"Then why don't we get back there?"

"Because there ain't anything there, that's why."

"But the *San Simon* . . ."

". . . *Was* a treasure ship," Bud finished for him. "*Was,* Joie. You know what that means? It means somebody else got that treasure a long time ago. It's on another wreck someplace out there and when we find that, we got the treasure. Now shut up. We've been movin' so fast we nearly got tricked."

"*Tricked?*"

Bud pointed toward the lines that etched the sandy bottom. "See that? Tracks, that's what they are. Those kids have cut back and are heading toward Peolle Is-

87

land. We never would've caught them if we followed these tracks here.''

Joie nodded eagerly. "Think we can do it now?"

"Yeah," Bud told him. "Now. They probably think they have plenty of time and they'll be slowing down. So we speed up."

Joie wiped the sweat from his face and was eager to get started. He had a better nose than his brother and he wanted to tell Bud how it was beginning to smell funny and the color of the sky was strange, but he didn't want Bud taking a poke at him. Whenever Bud had something on his mind, he couldn't think of anything else. Joie was wishing the visibility were better in the east. Someplace out there the sea was just doing something, but it sure was waiting to come back, and when it did, nobody had better be in its way.

That yell of Petey Betts had reached the boys too and when they had inched up a sandslope as far as they dared, they could see its source and all the other islanders descending upon it.

"Do you think . . . they really found it?" Josh asked curiously.

"Probably. All the other known wrecks have been located; the *San Simon* was the last. It sure must have been pretty well hidden."

"There, my friend"—Josh smiled—"is where you will see one big fight pretty soon. From now on, everybody on Peolle and Ara will be enemies." He stopped, looked sharply at Larry and asked, "You think those Jimson brothers could have heard that cry?"

"Why not? We did."

"Then maybe they would . . ."

Larry shook his head. "They wouldn't waste their time. I think they know very little will be on that wreck to start with. What they *really* want is to stop us. We're the ones who stand between them and the fresh air now. Jail is their next step if we make it back to the island."

"Don't say *if*, Larry."

"Okay. *When* we get back."

7 For the past hour, Captain Stephen Morelli had kept the *Emory Welsch* on a steady course with depth soundings being given him at five-minute intervals. Each report was checked against the navigational charts by his mate, Doug Andrews, and radioed in to the Coast Guard at Miami.

There was no doubt about it now. The charts were right and the sea was wrong. A whole section of it seemed to have picked itself up and simply disappeared. Until an hour ago, the depth change had grown more noticeable, the sea bottom steadily inching up toward them; then suddenly there was no change and the last few reports seemed to indicate a swing in the opposite direction.

Doug Andrews looked up from his charts, his eyes tired. "The last readings show a five percent rise, sir. Another thirty minutes and we'll know for sure."

"Any confirmations from other ships?"

Doug fingered through the top few radio communications beside him. "We're the outside ship, Captain. If there's any change, we'll feel it first."

"This can be bad news, Mr. Andrews. If there's any sudden return of the ocean, the shorelines will be swept clean."

"They should have time to evacuate, sir."

"Perhaps the mainlands, but the islands will be devastated."

"If there is no wild tidal action," Doug suggested, "nothing might change at all. It might come back as quietly as it left."

"Does that sound logical, Mr. Andrews?"

The mate had to concede that it didn't. He had been at sea long enough to know how perverse nature could be when she wanted to. And right then, nature had a strange look. She was too quiet and very strangely colored, and when he stood outside in the breeze, she even smelt funny.

A runner from the radio shack entered and handed the mate a radio form. The Coast Guard was getting depth soundings from other ships now and caution was being urged for all ships in the area. Evacuation of the coastline population in endangered areas was already

91

under way and an attempt was being made by military air and naval forces to alert people in remote areas of the possible hazard.

At the wheel, the young sailor looked anxiously at the skipper. Out of the corner of his eye, Captain Morelli caught his unspoken concern and said softly, "Keep a steady course, helmsman."

"Aye, sir."

The Captain looked at the seaman beside the Fathometer. "Any further depth change?"

"Still holding fast, sir."

"Mr. Andrews . . ."

"Yes, Captain?"

"Get a couple of men to throw sounding leads from the port and starboard bows."

The mate glanced at him quizzically, saying nothing.

"Too often, electronic equipment can be affected by natural disturbances," the Captain explained. "A manual check will make any instrument change positive."

Doug Andrews nodded, relayed the order to a pair of seamen and waited for their report. In fifteen minutes he had it. The manual measurement matched the depth readings on the fathometer. The only instrument that showed any noticeable difference was the thermometer. It was getting chillier than it should have been.

And now, a new silence seemed to have captured the ship. There were no jolting voices to be heard, no singing, and the only activities of the men off watch was staring at the strangely colored sky and listening anxiously to overhear any later news from the bridge. The pair in the bow throwing the leaded weights forward, letting the lines go out, then hauling them in to measure the lengths, had plenty of runners ready to relay the depth soundings to the Captain, eager to have anything to do during this strange day at sea.

Although nothing *appeared* changed since there was nothing to compare it with, everyone knew that the vast expanse of the Atlantic Ocean had shifted into a new configuration, and whether it was for good or for bad no one could tell . . . they could only hope.

The unnatural quiet wasn't only on the *Emory Welsch*. It hung over the thousands of people lining the beaches of Florida and the heavily populated islands to the south. It was the quiet of terror, the moment of facing the unknown and being unable to cry or scream for relief.

They heard the news first as a rumor . . . the sea was coming back in! A tremor went through the crowd, ears alert, waiting for further news. Every radio was tuned to the newscast, and the initial announcement of the new development gave the crowd an uneasy feeling. Some in the rear started edging back as if they expected a huge wave to engulf the whole coast, and here and there in the midst of the throng, others got the same idea.

Sergeant Arthur Lander of the Miami police was in

charge of a command post where the crowd was thickest and he saw the first change in the attitude of people gathered on the edge of the ocean. He picked up the microphone in his radio car and hit the button.

"Lander here at post ten."

"Go ahead, Lander."

"Did you get a news flash on the tide?"

"Rodger, Lander. Coast Guard has reported a shift in the sea flow. All indications show it coming back in."

"They make a public announcement?"

There was a moment's pause, then: "Just a few minutes ago."

Sergeant Lander made a grunting sound of annoyance and said, "I thought so. They should have notified us first. You'd better alert all command posts to stand by. This bunch down here looks like they're going to break and run for it."

"Anything happening now?"

Lander shook his head. "Not yet, but if a couple of people suddenly get hysterical and try to cut out they'll start a panic like you never saw before in your life. It'll be worse than yelling 'Fire!' in a theater."

Again there was silence; then the base said, "We'll route some more cars your way, Sergeant. We'll institute all mob and panic control routines as best we can. Each command post will be on its own, however. It's a situation we never had to face before, so good luck."

"Yeah, swell," Sergant Lander said before he tossed the mike back on its hook. But the Sergeant was a good professional cop and didn't waste any time. In his mind he recognized all the possibilities and called his men together. In five minutes the orders were given, all the equipment issued and the police assigned their positions. If they were lucky, they might be able to handle any sudden surge of the huge crowd.

It was a big *if*.

Like most radio shops, Bill Andra's had a receiver set to police frequency and when Ladner ended his communication, Bill looked at Vincent Damar, his face pale. "If there's panic . . . ," he started to say.

Vincent held up his hand. "Don't speak about it."

"It could happen, Vince."

"Yes, I know. If one person flips out and screams or tries to run, it'll trigger the entire lot of them. It'll be a regular stampede and who knows how many will get killed in the rush. I hope the police have enough manpower to handle it."

"What about those areas where there are no cops?"

This time it was Vincent who went colorless. His mind was back at the island where his son was alone, and he was envisioning the worst. At least here they could go inland for safety, but on the smaller islands, there was no "inland."

"Look, Vince," Bill said, "don't sweat it too soon. So far there's no trouble at all, at least not from the water. Larry could be safer where he is than if he were caught in a mob scene here."

"Yeah, I know, Bill, but . . ."

Before he could get any further the door burst open and a big, tanned, burly guy came in totally out of breath and shoved a carton onto Bill's workbench. "You gotta help me, Bill," the guy said.

"Sure, Johnny . . . what's the trouble?"

"We're all set to go up in the chopper when the RB-510 went dead. And I mean dead. Started smoking, so I yanked it out of the panel and you got to do something, Bill."

"Come on, Johnny, I can't fix a radio in ten minutes."

"I know. That's why I want to borrow yours. Bill, I have to get that radio in. I got a contract to take this newsman south and without the RB-510 I'm shot down. He'll never get his story back and I lose a bundle of money."

"How far south, Johnny?" There was something quietly inquisitive in Bill's voice.

"The guy wants to range down to Triske Island."

"Isn't that past Peolle?" Bill asked him.

"Yeah, why?"

"How many you carrying?"

"Just the newsman."

"That chopper of yours seats four, doesn't it?"

"Uh-huh."

Bill looked at Vince and grinned. He said to Johnny, "I'll lend you my RB-510 if you drop my buddy off at Peolle."

The big flier didn't bother to argue. He just nodded, grinned and said, "It's a deal. Gimme the radio."

Five minutes later Vincent was in Johnny's truck, cradling the radio in his lap. In another half-hour they'd be in the air and on the way to Peolle Island.

Now it was all a matter of time, and every minute seemed an eternity.

"How far ahead do you think they are, Bud?"

The older Jimson brother paused and studied the footprints in the sand. Now the outlines were becoming more clear-cut and fresh-looking, and although the two men were tiring, Bud realized that little by little they were getting closer to the boys. He stood up and searched the area ahead, but there were too many sand hillocks in the way and with the strange orange setting sun in his eyes, he couldn't make out anything discernible more than a few hundred yards ahead.

Mentally, he measured the distance between themselves and Peolle Island. When they caught the kids they'd still have to be out of sight of any of the islanders, so that meant they'd have to make contact before the kids reached the weeds a quarter-mile offshore.

Bud's mean eyes squinted when he thought of the pleasure he'd have when his hands would be around their necks. Where he caught them was where they would stay, shoved well down under the sand where the sea life would gradually take any sign that they ever existed at all. It would just be a case of a couple of stupid kids who strayed away into the ocean when they should

97

have stayed home. After that he and Joie'd have plenty of time to take care of Vincent Damar and the secret he had.

Joie said, "Well?"

"They can't be more than a half-mile ahead. They're going slower now."

"How can ya tell?"

"Because the space between their footprints is getting smaller," Bud explained. "The tracks aren't filling in so fast any more."

"You think it'll be soon, Bud?"

"It'll be soon, Joie," his brother told him, looking at him with disgust. It would be nice to leave stupid Joie out here with the kids, too, he thought. Having him around all the time was like dragging an anchor. "Come on," he said, and the both of them picked up the pace again, paralleling the tracks laid down by Larry and Josh.

A fresh wind whipped across the wet sand and the men both shivered momentarily. It was an odd, disturbing wind, much too cool for this time of year, and riding on it were voices from a couple of miles away, voices so clear they could recognize their owners, voices yelling and screaming from the covered wreck of the *San Simon*.

They had to take a chance and make their way to the top of the highest outcropping in the area. Unless they got a clear fix on their destination, they could wander off course and lose precious time in getting home to safety. The trouble was that they'd be exposing themselves dangerously if they were within sighting distance of their trackers.

"What do you think, Josh?"

"Back there," Josh said, "I think we gave them the slip."

"They aren't too dumb, though. At least, not Bud."

Josh looked at the sky again. The sun seemed to be buried behind an orangy-red haze and he couldn't be certain of its position at all. "We have to make sure, Larry."

"Okay, let's go. We'll stay in front of the crest and let it cover us as much as possible." He felt a chill go over him when the new wind hit his skin and he frowned, not liking what he felt. "Something's dif-ferent, Josh."

His friend knew what he meant and nodded. "I feel it, too."

Quickly, they looked at each other, both with the same thought. "The sea is coming back in," Larry said softly.

And then it stopped being just a thought. It was something they both knew. Absolutely, definitely *knew*. They could hear the voices from far off, heard Jake Skiddo and Petey Betts trying to defend their find without any luck, the other voices mocking them, and Josh said, "I wonder if they know, too."

But it wouldn't be likely. That bunch would be much too concerned with scrabbling for gold or anything valuable they could carry to recognize any change in the situation at all. And behind them, the Jimsons would be too concerned with *them* to consider what was happening.

Maybe.

So they got in front of the slope, helped each other up the loose sand and finally positioned themelves so they had an almost direct westerly view. For a good minute they sat there, knowing that if they didn't proceed carefully, the terror would get to them too.

They had expected to see Peolle Island. What they did *see* was a golden haze that obscured any physical objects more than a half-mile away.

"We could be too far south," Larry suggested.

Josh studied the terrain in front of them a good while before he was certain; then he pointed slightly to the right and said, "There, Larry. A point we passed earlier . . . where Pierre Combolt's two-masted schooner sank. We were north of it."

"You sure, Josh?"

"Yes, I remember it well. Peolle lies a little to our right. If we hurry, we can be at the island well before dark."

Larry nodded and began to ease himself back to the bottom. For the second time, both the boys were beginning to realize just how tired they were. Had they not been going at such a forced pace, they would have been fine; the past hours were telling on them now. They were hungry, they were thirsty and their bodies were aching from the ordeal. All they could hope for was that their pursuers were feeling the same strains of the chase as they were.

And up to that point, their pursuers *were* being beaten down. Bud and Joie Jimson were too tired to bother speaking to each other and their breath came in hard, hot gasps. A wetness had encompassed the area a few hundred yards back and the footprints they had been following were completely obliterated for a while, and it had taken them thirty minutes of fast cross-tracking before they picked up the prints again.

Twice Joie had stumbled and they had to rest to get their strength back, and by the time they found the trail again, they had been ready to assume the boys had gotten too far ahead for them to catch, but just at that moment Joie's mouth went slack and he pointed straight ahead. Bud followed the line of sight and felt the strength flow back into his body.

Ahead, on the crest of a hillock, clearly outlined against the sun was something that moved . . . and the only thing that could possibly move out there would be the target they were after.

"We got them now," Bud said.

His brother finally got his breath back. "They got to be tired, too."

Bud nodded his agreement. "Now we really push. They don't know we're here, so we got the edge on our side."

"You think it'll be long?"

"Another hour," Bud told him. "Then we got 'em."

101

Miles away, north of Peolle, a helicopter was taking off from its pad on the outskirts of Miami. It, too, was racing against time. From its cockpit an aerial broadcast of conditions on the sea below was being transmitted, the commentator giving a running account of what he was seeing, making the most of the last of daylight.

But to Vincent Damar, time was moving much too slowly. Even though he was airborne now, and enroute to Peolle Island, the slow speed of the chopper infuriated him. Inside himself was a knowledge too, and no matter what his friend Bill Andra had told him, he *knew* something was wrong back there on Peolle.

Yes, something was very drastically wrong.

8 The Miami police were lucky. The raw power of the bullhorns had kept the panic of the mob in check whenever unruly incidents started to appear, but it was the silent wonder in the minds of each person, the awe of the unknown, that really made them disperse without any difficulty. In the northern part of the state the water had already seeped back, rising slowly without causing any damage, but in outlying areas, this was to be expected.

It hadn't been until the last hour that the American Naval base at Guantànamo on the tip of Cuba had released news of the severity of the tidal drop. More than two dozen boats were stranded miles offshore, but so far there had been no reports of casualties.

But there was one alarming fact that seemed to go unnoticed. Although the ships at sea were beginning to radio the new changes in bottom depths, there was little visible sign that the sea was coming back in any great rush. What did get reported and was entirely overlooked was the degree of wetness in the formerly almost-dried ocean bottom. Two transmissions from ham radio operators in the southern islands relayed the message that the sand was getting soupy and dangerous, as if the ocean were trying to come back underground.

Not everyone was unaware of this fact, however. Hovering over the empty ocean bed, Victor Damar noticed the wet-shiny fingers on the sand, like unseen rivers making new paths toward the far-off shoreline. His mind could undersand certain scientific principles that might cause this new condition, but it only added to his concern for his son's safety. Nature could work at incredible speeds if she wanted to, without being deterred by man's desires at all. Every day, in some areas of the world, there were tides that ebbed and flowed at speeds no man could match on foot.

Two others suddenly noticed their feet sinking deeper into the sand, and Joie Jimson said, "Bud . . . it's getting soft."

"I can see that, jughead."

"It should be dry here. Why is it getting wet, Bud?"

"How should I know." He raised his hand for a halt and studied the terrain. The footprints of the boys

104

headed toward a hillock but were already beginning a swing to the right. "We're going to cut over that mound there and . . ."

"That's a lot of work, Bud!"

"So's sloshing through wet sand. If those kids stay in the muck they'll slow down even more. Now shut up and save your breath. You're going to need it going over those dunes."

"Come on, Bud . . ."

"You want a rap in the ear?" Bud demanded aggressively.

His brother shook his head.

"Then move it!" Bud told him.

Together, they started off again, weariness dragging on every muscle in their bodies. They didn't know it, but if they could have seen what was not too far ahead of them, they would have run at full speed with the reserve energy the sight of victory gives.

Larry and Josh were standing stock-still, looking at a scene they never could have imagined. When they had approached it from the other direction coming out, they had taken it for just another long rise in the bottom, a natural seagrass-topped formation, but from where they were they saw what the configuration really represented.

It was an old iron ship lying on it's side, half-buried in the sand, its coral-covered deckworks clearly discernible but invisible from a topside view. Boats must have passed over it a thousand times, but its position and the camouflage that time and tides had disguised it with, had made it just another section of the rolling bottom of the ocean.

It was too much for their curiosity. It was something that had to be seen a little closer. The fear of their pursuers was suddenly lost when they were under the overhang of the deck and could look up at the place where sailors once stood.

"How big do you think it is, Larry?"

Not all of the vessel was uncovered, but from the slope of her hull he was able to generalize as to the length. "A hundred eighty feet maybe. About an average size ship for those days."

"Would a ship this size have sailed this close to shore?"

"Only accidentally," Larry said quietly.

Josh caught the odd tone in his voice and his eyes searched for an answer.

"The ship wasn't under control," Larry told him. "There was a mutiny on board, they were drifting and when the boilers blew, it went down away from the regular shipping channel."

"How do you know this, Larry?"

Larry kicked at the coral that covered most of the old steel nameplate that was fastened to the top of what was the pilothouse. Part of the engraved "E" was visible, and when a large plate of coral calcium dropped loose, the word *"Belle"* stood out large and clear. "Under the sand is the rest of the name, Josh. We're looking at the wreck of the *Nantucket Belle!"*

Josh's face was a mask of astonishment. "You mean . . . the one your father . . . ?"

Larry nodded. "The *real* treasure ship. The one that salvaged the gold and jewels from the *San Simon* so many years ago."

Silently, they stood there a minute: then Josh said, "When the sea went out it sucked all the sand from this almost-upside-down ship."

A funny little grin crossed Larry's mouth. "And when it comes back it might fill it up again."

"Maybe the sand will cover it so we'll never find it again."

"That's right," Larry agreed, "so maybe we ought to take a look inside while we have the chance."

"Do you . . . think it will be safe?"

"We'll have to be very careful."

But the closer they got, the more they began to regret their decision. There was something eerie about that old ship. Somewhere on board would be the bones of men who had gone down with her, and the others who were killed in the fight over the great riches not one of them ever got. There were sea creatures who made homes in the crusty caverns of old wrecks and some could still be hiding in the dark, wet corners of the hulk, terrified by the change in their surroundings and ready to attack anything that moved.

But it was something they had to do. Larry and his father had searched long and hard to locate this very ship and here was an opportunity to explore it under conditions that might never occur again. *If only his dad were here, Larry thought.* For a second his mind flicked back to the Jimson brothers and he mentally computed the time lapse between them. If he and Josh hurried, he figured, they could cover a good section of any interior that was exposed and get out with plenty of time to make it to shore. If they were lucky, they might even find the treasure!

Larry never figured it for a vain thought at all. He never considered that the treasure could have been scattered all over the ocean in the violence of the sinking, nor the possibility that hundreds of tons of sand might still cover it somewhere deep within the bowels of the hull. He was so full of the adventure and enthusiasm only young boys know that he completely dismissed all ideas of danger or failure and laughed out loud. He and Josh climbed up the rise of sand that led to the vacant windows of the pilothouse and wriggled inside its barely lighted interior.

Neither of them noticed the long, wet fingers of sand that were beginning to develop behind them, snaking around the hillocks, reaching out and growing, seeming to follow underground paths of new rivers.

When their eyes became accustomed to the gloom they took a good look around them. At first, it was difficult to realize where they were; not having any outside reference, they seemed to be sticking out from the wall of the pilothouse.

Larry knew what vertigo was and explained it to Josh. "Don't worry about what it looks like . . . just figure that whatever you're standing on is the bottom no matter which way the ship is tilted."

"I feel like a fly on the ceiling," Josh replied. He

looked up at the way the brass binnacle and the crusted ship's wheel were pointed down at him from an angle.

Small pieces of old wreckage were sticking out of the sand . . . the remains of a stool, part of the iron framework from a window and a twisted and bent brass megaphone. The boys realized there was no time to look for souvenirs and when they made certain the area was devoid of anything important, they clambered out again, got on the topside of the pilothouse, worked their way aft, then dropped to a stanchion, where they stood long enough to get their bearings.

It was strange walking along a ship that was lying on its side. And even more than on its side, because the deck itself was covering them and they had a feeling that if they let go, they'd sail off into the sky. But the sensation finally cured itself and they went from one foothold to another until they had crossed the forward deck area and were standing on the raised housing amidships, looking down into smashed and open portholes.

Inside, it looked gloomier than ever and a chill swept over both boys when the thought of entering faced them. Oh, it wouldn't be any trouble to get inside at all. Right beside them the bulkhead door was twisted open and rusted solidly in that gaping position, an invitation for anyone who had the nerve to enter.

Ragged edges of metal projected out of the framework that had held the door, eroded into gnarled, deadly points. "This ship," Josh said, "looks like she wants to eat us."

"Scared?"

Josh nodded. "You?"

"I sure am," Larry said, "but if we don't go in, later I'll be more mad than I am scared."

"You're crazy, you know?"

"Aren't we both?"

"Sure looks like it. My father, man, right now he'd be telling me to forget this crazy thing and get out fast."

Larry shrugged, walked over and squatted down beside the open door in the bulkhead. "There's just about enough light left to make a quick search."

"Then let's hurry," Josh said.

Larry took a deep breath, then gently let himself ease down into the opening, careful of the steel teeth on either side of him. When he dropped off into the sand he stepped aside and watched while Josh's figure was framed in the open door a moment before landing beside him.

They had expected an unusual quiet in this weird underwater tomb, but it wasn't so at all. The wind was making shrill whistling noises passing across holes where rivets had popped out of the hull. Strange crackling sounds of hard shells brushing together made them take note that this was an *inhabited* place. Things were here, hiding in darkness and lurking just under the sand . . . things with needlelike points and harsh, crushing claws.

"I wish we had a flashlight, Josh."

"Me . . . I wish we were home." Josh half-tripped over something partially buried in the sand, reached down and extracted an old blackened copper pot with a

112

two-foot handle. "It isn't much, but in case we need a weapon . . ."

"Against what?"

"Whatever lives here," Josh said. "Tell me, where are we on this ship?"

"Some sort of a stateroom or saloon. The *Nantucket Belle* was fitted to carry passengers and this would have been their dining area. If we go aft a little, there should be a stairwell going to the quarters below . . . only in this case, we won't be going down at all . . . we'll be going parallel to the bottom."

"You're thinking of something, aren't you?"

Larry nodded. Finally he said, "If there was any treasure, it would have been kept under guard by the Captain. Now . . . when the crew staged that mutiny it had to be an attack on the officers, but the ship blew up so fast it's doubtful if anybody ever laid hands on the treasure."

"Then . . . the Captain would have it in his cabin?"

"Or some other strongroom."

"We shall see, Larry. But let's hurry."

The stairwell was right where Larry had expected it to be and he was grateful that the ship was lying the way it was. The wooden steps had long ago been eaten away be teredo worms, and the two boys made their way toward the lower deck by simply walking along the steel wall.

Light was filtering down, making it brighter than

113

they expected, but it wasn't until they reached the vertical barrier—actually the floor of the deck below—that they knew what caused it. The separation in the hull where the force of the boiler explosion had ripped the steel plates apart was letting the sunlight in. Ordinarily the opening wouldn't be visible at all, the weed barrier that grew upright in the sea water hiding the huge gap completely. But now the grass hung against the steel, damp and limp, outlining a jagged skylight.

"We're in luck again, Josh. We can see."

"I hope we like what we see," Josh said. "This isn't too good." He was indicating the evenly spaced holes in the "floor" ahead of them.

"Those are stateroom doors," Larry explained. "Don't forget, we're standing on the wall now."

After taking a good look, Josh asked, "Most of this ship is buried under the sand, isn't it?"

"I think so," Larry said glumly.

"Then if there is no sand inside, and we can find a way to get down farther, we'll really be far below the bottom of the sea, is that so?"

"Yeah, you're right, but don't plan on doing it. This old steel hull could still hold water, so even if there's no sand, we're inside a big basin of water."

"And no SCUBA gear," Josh said, grinning.

"Aren't we lucky," Larry laughed back. "Come on, let's see what we can find."

They had to help each other into the first two compartments, then stand until their eyes accepted the deeper gloom. Both places held the obvious remains of brass beds and scraps of what appeared to have been hand luggage. The walls and floor, being of steel, were still intact although well rusted and, in most places, coral-encrusted.

To get in the third compartment, both of them had to sit on the wall and kick at the door with their feet until the latch broke and the light metal door creaked on its hinges and slowly was driven back until there was room for the boys to drop down inside.

In this place there was no sand at all. Broken pieces of furniture were still recognizable for what they were and the broken bed lay piled in a corner. From the ruined door above, the filtered light came down with that strange orange glow and the boys were about to dismiss the place as being empty.

They turned, got ready to reach for the sill overhead . . . and they both froze with a sudden terror. They were being watched! From the murky shadows two grinning skulls were gaping at them, lying in a scattered pile of bones that hadn't moved since they had fallen there, the skeleton outlines of the bodies partially hidden under scraps of leather or heavy cloth, the bony hands of each still clutching the hilt of an old cutlass.

When he could talk, Josh said, "One must have been a mutineer. They fought to the death."

"But the bones . . . they're not disturbed."

"The door was closed on them, but there was no wave action and no sea life to bother them."

"But . . . shouldn't we have seen other . . . remains?"

115

"Nothing lasts long underwater. Nothing that once was alive, anyway."

Larry took the copper pot from Josh and pushed it among the wreckage, but there was nothing of importance at all, so he indicated that they should get back in the passageway again.

With a lift up, Josh grabbed the sill and hauled himself out of the room, then lay on his stomach and grabbed Larry's outstretched hand. A quick pull while Larry pushed against the doorjamb and they were on their feet.

Now there was a more somber mood to the moment. Never before had either of the boys seen the bones of dead men and knowing they were likely to find even more made their bodies draw tight with nervous tension. In a way, as with the old submarine they had discovered, they were again at a tomb. No . . . not *at* but *in* it, with the dead of all those years ago.

Neither of them wanted to show anxiety, so Larry suggested they try the rest of the rooms off the hall and call it quits if they didn't find anything. Josh went along with the idea and they didn't waste any time. Getting back under the open sky was something to look forward to.

There was another room closed shut, but this time they couldn't open the door far enough to squeeze through. From what they could see, it was no different from the others, and if there were any relics of dead bodies in there, they were out of sight.

It was the last room that was different. It was twice

as large as the others, the midwall being gone, so that the room went across to where it opened into the opposite corridor. Only in this case, the other corridor wasn't really *across* any more . . . it was down, and in the dim light the boys could see the gleam of water below them.

"This could have been the Captain's quarters," Larry said.

"No good," Josh reflected.

"Why not?"

"The crew would have broken in and looted it."

"Think so?" Larry asked. "Look at the door again. See those dents in the metal?" He indicated at least a dozen four-inch scars on the panel, and in at least two cases the ends of the dents had opened into the metal. "Somebody used an ax trying to break in."

"How do you know they didn't?"

"Because we had to kick that rusted latch open to get in ourselves."

"Do you think . . ."

Larry shrugged. "We'll have to find out."

For a minute the boys thought it was a lost cause; then Josh suggested, "Those old beds back there, Larry. They had fronts and backs like a ladder. They weren't rusted, so they must have been made of brass . . ."

"Right! We could hook them together and . . . Come on, let's get them!"

They were so enthused by the project that everything else left their minds. It didn't take long at all to get out the metal sections of the beds and arrange a make-

117

shift ladder by hooking the frames together. When they were sure the arrangement would hold their weight, they grinned at each other with pleasure and Josh, being lighter, let himself down first.

What neither of them noticed was that the sun's rays were shifting and it wasn't as light as it had been, and more time had passed since they entered the hull of the *Nantucket Belle* than they thought.

9 At first Bud Jimson figured the kids had taken a wrongly angled path and would cut back north and he and Joie could save time by short-cutting the route. There shouldn't have been any reason at all why the kids would want to climb over that big mound off to the left. He was all ready to follow his plan when something about that mound made him look twice. He didn't have to do it again.

"What is it, Bud?"

He pointed. "What do you see there?"

"Only a . . ." Joie started to say. Then: "That's a ship!"

119

"We almost missed it."

"But . . ."

"See where the tracks go, Joie?"

His brother frowned and nodded; then he looked up, grinning evilly. "We got 'em, Bud. We sure got 'em good, all buttoned up inside a dead ship."

Bud's grin was just as evil. "Now we can make 'em part of a dead crew . . . and no way anybody's ever gonna find what happened to 'em."

They were terrified, all of them. Most were halfway up to their knees in wet sand, barely able to walk, and the whole ocean bottom to the east was starting to glisten. Miles away the setting sun was doing a sparkling dance off something very familiar to them and nobody had to tell them what was happening.

The sea was returning!

Gone were the pieces of junk they had scrounged out of the pile of ballast rock and rotted timbers that had been the *San Simon*. Nothing was of value that would drag them deeper into the sand. Without exception, all were clawing their way toward that distant spot on the horizon that was Ara Island, hoping they would make it in time. A quarter-mile ahead the bottom still showed itself to be dry, and if they could only get that far, their chances would improve.

On the side of the wreck, Jake Skiddo and Petey Betts were trying to right the dune buggy. They shoved and heaved, finally getting it back on its wheels again, and they clambered aboard. Petey gave Jake a dirty look and said, "You watch what you're doing, y'hear?"

"Oh, shut up and hang on."

Jake hit the gas, and with a jolting rush the buggy jounced down the pile of rocks, hit the bottom, and the mud cleats clawed for traction. For a few seconds it didn't look as though they were going to make it; then the buggy pushed loose and began a crawl toward Ara, gradually picking up speed as it went. They passed a few of the others that were fighting through the sand but ignored their pleas for a ride. All they were concerned about were their own skins and nothing was going to stop them.

Nothing, that is, except a sinkhole in the soft sand. One second they were riding. The next they were splashing their way out of the sand-soupy puddle that was swallowing the dune buggy. Bitter about their luck, they joined the others, wading mightily toward shore to keep from being gobbled up by an angry sea.

From the chopper, Vincent Damar could see the silvery sheen of the Atlantic, the sun glinting off it like diamonds. They were at five thousand feet and the sky was brighter here than at ground level, with less of that strange orange tint.

Occasionally they passed over small boats that had been left stranded on the bottom, their captains and mates still with them. Most were chartered fishing boats and they were too far off shore for their crews to attempt

121

a walk back. Apparently they were simply awaiting a return of the tide to float them and as long as they still had radio contact, they weren't too worried.

The pilot of the chopper was in constant communication with ships at sea and the Coast Guard base and as far as could be determined, there still was no damage. Ships lying well offshore had already recorded a four-foot rise in depth from their lowest point and the coastline cities were breathing with relief in the northern sectors because the basins were filling up and very little damage had been experienced anywhere.

But farther south the question was still unanswered. The oceanography services were being canvased to get their opinion, but as yet none was forthcoming. Although the ocean had receded quickly and passively to the north, in the south it could sweep back with a rush that could destroy anything in its path. There was no way anyone could form an opinion, for what everyone was seeing was something that hadn't happened before in the written history of America.

Vincent Damar kept watching below, eyes anxiously searching the east where the sea lurked, coming back at a still-undetermined speed. The bottom was uneven, so the major depths would be filled in first without too much forward motion, but when the bottom leveled off and the sea reached the shelf, that forward motion could be increased a hundredfold. There was just no way of telling what it was going to do.

The pilot reached over and tapped Vincent on the shoulder, then pointed ahead toward the horizon.

"Peolle Island," he said. "We'll be there in twenty-five minutes."

"Any radio from the island at all?"

"None."

Vincent Damar looked at his hands. They were knotted into tight fists. There wasn't any doubt about it in his mind at all . . . his son was somewhere on that vast reach of wet sand, and getting ready to engulf him was that shiny, silvery ocean in the background.

The boys took a deep breath of relief. The water around their feet was only about four inches deep. When they had dropped from their makeshift ladder they had only been able to guess at the distance and had figured no more than a foot. Had it been any more, they would have had trouble reaching the ladder to get back out again.

The rubble of the room lay about their feet, rotted wood and more metal, rusted and bent out of shape. But not all the metal was indistinguishable. Josh saw a handle projecting from the silt, worked it loose and came up with a cry of triumph. "A mug, Larry . . . look, it's silver!"

Larry took it from him, turned it over and rubbed some of the muck off its surface. "It's silver, all right. Luckily it was stuck there alone. If it had been in contact with any other metal it would have oxided."

"Like that clump of metal we found on the beach . . . the one that used to be silver coins?"

123

"Exactly." Under the heel of his hand Larry could feel lines on the mug and scrubbed a little harder. After a minute he held it in the fading light and studied what he saw. "We're in the Captain's cabin, that's for sure. This was his cup. Look at this."

His finger underlined the printed *"Captain Henry Logan, Nantucket Belle."*

And as though that were a hidden signal, both the boys felt a cold, clammy sensation and looked to their left. The skull was near what had once been a metal table. It was grinning like the others, although nothing was funny at all. Around the bony forehead was a metal band that used to be part of a cap, still attached to it the brass insignia of master's rank. A small salt water crayfish was crawling out of one empty eye socket, waving its antennae in the air.

And the Captain himself was there to greet them, the remnants of two pistols still lying there among the bones of his hands.

"He was waiting for them to break his door down," Larry said.

"But the sea got them all," Josh added. He tore his eyes away from the gleaming skull, peering into the gloom of the room's corners. "Could there be anything here?"

"It'll be on the bottom if there is. Why don't you take one side and I'll take the other. See what we can find."

Two minutes later they met at the forward wall. "Nothing," Josh said. "How about you?"

Larry was about to shake his head, then stopped.

124

"Look at this." He wiped at what had looked like a plain wall panel.

"What is it?"

"A door." He saw Josh's surprised look and added, "Don't forget, we're standing on the *wall*. This part of the door is its *bottom*."

"Crazy, man."

"Give me a hand. Let's see if we can get it open."

It didn't take much prying. The handle of the copper pot Josh had kept with him made short work of the latch, and their feet did the rest of it. The door flew off, breaking at the hinges, clattering noisily across the room. Inside was a small area, piled with pieces of what once had been boxes of tools still recognizable heaped where they had fallen when the ship went down.

Even now, there was so much loose debris under their feet that the boys could hardly walk. "What is that stuff, Larry?"

"Beats me." Larry bent down, scooped up a couple of golf-ball-sized objects and said, "One's a hunk of coal. The other looks like a rock."

"Coal? In here?"

There was just enough light seeping in for them to see it, a section of the side that was decking when the ship had been upright having been wrenched loose and bent out. "The boiler explosion," Larry explained. "It blew coal from the bunkers right through the wall." He tossed the chunk of coal back and stuck the other rock in his pocket. "I'll keep this souvenir with the other rocks in my tropical fish aquarium."

"You got more rocks in there now than you need."

Gently, they picked their way forward, stepping carefully. Then Josh tripped, nearly fell and caught himself just in time.

"Trouble?"

Josh shook his head and reached down to his feet. He let his hands run across the objects that he had stumbled over, then drew back as if they were hot. "Larry . . . come here."

"What have you got?"

"Feel here . . . at my feet."

Larry's hands went under the water; then he touched the smooth, cold oblong objects, moved one, finally got it tilted enough to get his fingers under it, then came up slowly, the small object a massive weight in his hands.

They didn't have to be told what it was. Even after having been under water all those years, the yellow sheen was still there. Nothing else that small could have weighed that much . . . and in Larry's hands was the wealth of a lifetime.

With the same breath, the boys said, *"Gold!"*

They had found the treasure!

But the excitement of their discovery faded to nothing compared with the incredible terror that came with the sound behind them, a harsh metallic sound they both recognized at once. As though it were nothing but junk, Larry threw the gold bullion down and they scrambled for the door of the room. They made it together, just in time to see their "ladder" being pulled up out of sight.

They had found gold, all right, but the Jimson's had

126

found them! They knew it when they heard Bud's harsh laughter and the stupid giggle from his brother, Joie.

For a stunned second all the boys could imagine was that they were trapped, sealed in a dead ship with dead men they would soon join. Only now did they realize the time they had used and sense how low the sun was by the dim light.

Above them they could hear the feet of the Jimson brothers treading the steel, heading forward. There were no more tracks to follow. They had ended at the *Nantucket Belle* and once more that nasty laugh rang through the tomb of the ship like a hollow echo.

"Larry . . ." Josh was looking down at his legs. The water wasn't inches deep any more. It was closer to his knees now.

"The sea is coming back in," Larry said.

"We could float out," Josh suggested.

"By then it will be dark. No . . . we have to get out now or we'll never make it."

"I'm afraid, my friend, that it won't be. There's no way we can reach that door up there, not even if I stood on your shoulders."

"But there's a way, pal."

Josh looked at him hopefully. "Where?"

"The next room," Larry said. "You know that hole the explosion blew in . . . where the coal came from?"

"It goes into the next room . . . the one we already explored."

"You can get through, Josh. You're small enough."

Suddenly it dawned on him what Larry was suggesting. "No! Larry, without you . . ."

"Don't be stupid, Josh. If I can't get out at least you might be able to find something to help get me up, understand?"

The logic of it calmed Josh down and he nodded his agreement. Together, they went back to the small room, shoved their way to the rip in the plating; then Larry helped Josh up. He had to twist and squirm, but he made the other side. "Try it, Larry," Josh said. "You might make it."

"It's pretty small, Josh."

"Try it anyway! Here, give me your hand." He felt Larry's fingers lace around his wrist and hung on. He could see the effort his friend was putting out, the way he was trying to force himself through the narrow opening. The metal had already scraped Larry's skin and for a minute it didn't look as though he was going to make it, but with one last effort, flattening himself as much as possible, with Josh hauling on his arm, Larry broke through the slot and lay gasping for breath in front of Josh.

There wasn't time to waste gathering strength. They had to use what they had left. Someplace above them, the Jimson brothers would be plotting the position of the *Nantucket Belle* and they would have to get away from them unnoticed. The sand was dry enough outside, the hillocks getting smaller, so they would be fair game if they were chased by the larger men. No . . . now it would be stealth that counted . . . if they were lucky.

Unlike on their entry, this time the boys made as little noise as possible. They picked their way back care-

fully and when they reached the end of the corridor, the voices of the Jimson's came to them. Quietly, the boys edged back into the large saloon compartment, spotted the Jimson brothers and held themselves motionless until the men moved on past their position.

When they were sure they were clear, Larry and Josh squirmed through a section that had been wrenched out, stood there looking down, then made the eight-foot jump into the damp sand. Except for the *whoosh* of their breath when they landed, there was no noise at all. Larry nodded for Josh to follow him, scuttled forward on all fours, got to the end of the ship and took one last look around.

He knew the Jimsons were close, all right, but at that moment they weren't to be seen.

"Now!" Larry whispered, and both boys took off in a fast sprint, heading toward Peolle Island as fast as their feet could carry them. The sand was still firm and the going flat and straight. Ahead was another small hillock and if they reached it, the projection might just be high enough to shield them for another hundreds yards or so. All Larry knew was that they needed a distance of at least two football fields between them and the Jimsons to keep from being caught.

Right then there was *one* football-field length between them . . . and that was all they were getting. They heard Joie Jimson's voice bellow out, "Bud . . . there they go . . . they're getting away!"

And Bud's coarse holler right behind him, "Get them . . . chase them, you dumbhead! We can't let them reach Peolle!"

Joie was closer than his brother and his feet were plowing against the sand as he took huge strides toward his quarry. "They won't get away," he called back.

Larry took a quick look over his shoulder. His heart sank and try as he could his legs wouldn't go any faster. Joie was right. He was fresher and quicker. They weren't going to get away after all. He could almost feel Joie's hand closing around his neck.

Vincent Damar ran from the chopper, shielding his face against the blinding sand the rotors threw up, and the chopper moved up and away. When it was clear, Vincent spotted the house and got there as quickly as he could.

His worst fears were realized. The house was empty. There was no note—nothing to tell him what had happened. Just a missing son who had given in to childish curiosity and roamed off into the unknown.

For Vincent it was the end of everything . . . his son lost to him, the boat gone, all his savings wiped out. He looked toward the still-empty ocean with dull eyes. Nothing was moving out there. Nothing at all. Another few minutes and darkness would close in, the sea not far behind.

Idly he flipped the radio on and set it to his common frequency. Steve Percy over on Ara was on the mike, talking fast to someone on the beach. Half of the bunch who had gone out on the ocean bottom that day were already back and the other half were in sight, struggling against the wet sand. Some of the stragglers

132

still a half-mile out were being helped back, their strength gone from the effort of wading through the muck. There were no casualties except a lot of bitterness and hard feelings and some kid named Oliver Creighton was having a fit because Jake Skiddo and Petey Betts had lost his dune buggy.

If the strong could barely make it, Vincent thought, how could a kid?

"Sar . . ."

Vincent heard the voice without realizing it was there.

It came again. "Sar?"

He spun around, startled, until he recognized Timothy, Josh's father. "Come on in, Tim."

"Thank you." There was a fear in his eyes. "Have you seen Larry?"

Vincent sensed what was coming. "No."

"He and Josh were together."

With a horrible sense of foreboding, they both looked out toward the sea.

"It has them, Vincent," Tim said.

Vincent put his arms around his friend's shoulder, leading him to a chair. Just for something to do he filled the coffeepot and put it on the stove. There wasn't much anticipation in his voice when he said, "All we can do is wait, Tim."

"Josh is so little."

"So is Larry, but they're smart."

"The sea is smarter," Tim said.

"All we can do is wait."

133

They were tiring now, their breath like fire in their chests, legs pulling as if they had weights attached to them. Behind them the Jimsons were shouting to each other, their voices coming closer and closer. Peolle was still a good mile away, a dull smudge on the horizon with the wild orange sun sinking down behind it. Even the chill in the air didn't help them, nor the ocean that was coming in so fast that you could smell its saltiness.

Another thirty seconds and the Jimsons would have their hands on them and it was hardly worthwhile running any longer. For a brief second both the boys wanted to give up completely; then they both saw the same thing at the same time.

Directly ahead of them was that long, narrow trench they had had to cross that morning, the one with the deadly occupant who was trapped in that channel, the one who would respond to any other sound and motion he could feel and tear it apart with mad predator teeth.

It was either the Jimsons or the shark and their only chance lay with that gruesome monster whose speed was incredible and whose aim would be perfect in the trap of that narrow valley in the ocean's floor. But if they could get across it before the shark reached them . . .

And it was that single thought that lent wings to their feet, so that for the last few yards the Jimsons didn't gain on them at all. With one final, great leap the boys dove headlong into the trench, their arms flailing with a last, desperate effort. They could almost feel the vibrations of the shark's charge; then their feet hit the incline on the other side and they were clambering up it as fast as possible while Bud's voice was shrieking hoarsely at Joie and when they looked back, Bud was holding onto his brother in near panic on the opposite bank while their eyes bugged out at the sight of a fif-teen-foot shark waiting directly below for them.

Across the trench, Larry and Josh were trotting away, knowing that there was no way the Jimsons could catch them now. All they had to do was beat out the return of the sea. The Jimsons knew it too. They knew they'd never be able to get back to Ara again without facing a prison sentence. Now, the only thing open to them was getting back to where their boat lay on its side in the wet sand. If they hurried, they might make it. After that it would be some dirty little village in some remote, forgotten island.

Vincent and Timothy heard the shouts from the beach and with a yell of pure joy they ran out side by side. There was so much hugging and backslapping that the boys couldn't get a word in, so they waited until after they had eaten and everybody had settled down before they began their story.

Outside, the sea had returned, not violently but as quietly as it had left, seeping up from the bottom and rolling in on the tide from the west. It was well into the night when all the questions had been asked and the answers given; then Larry had one of his own to ask. "But Dad," he said, "isn't there some way we can get to that treasure ship?"

"Sorry, son, but you never triangulated the position. It might take a long time to find it again."

"Not if you had the equipment . . ."

"That takes money, Larry, a lot of money. We haven't got it any longer. Now we have to give up the island . . . everything . . . and by the time I could get another stake, who knows what would have happened to the *Nantucket Belle?* Believe me, if I could finance an expedition, all of us would be rich, even the people on Ara. Between the artifacts on the *San Simon,* that old submarine and the *Belle* herself, this would be one prosperous area indeed."

"Too bad," Josh said.

"Too bad what?" Larry asked him.

"Too bad we didn't bring home one of those gold bars we found."

Larry let out a laugh. "That sure would have been great all right, but at least we came close. We *felt* the stuff." He reached in his pocket and brought out his rock. "And at least I have a souvenir. I hope my tropical fish enjoy it."

"What is it?" his father asked.

"Just a crazy-looking rock that was in that room." He tossed it to his father, who held the golf-ball-sized rock between his thumb and forefinger.

Vincent spun it around, looking at it casually and was about to toss it back when suddenly he frowned,

136

looked at it closer, then ran to his desk and pulled out a magnifying glass and studied the specimen carefully.

For some reason everyone in the room was strangely silent, as if waiting for something tremendous to happen. There was an electrical tingle touching all of them and as Vincent Damar's eyes began to light up, the tingling got even stronger.

Then he began to laugh. He laughed until the tears were rolling down his cheeks and the others were laughing too, even though they didn't know what they were laughing at.

Finally words came to young Larry and he said, "For pete's sake, Dad, what's the big joke?"

Vincent Damar wiped his eyes and put Larry's "rock" in the middle of the table. He looked at each boy in turn, then winked with pleasure at Timothy, telling him to get ready to be real proud of his son.

"Larry," he said, "that crazy rock of yours *is one of the biggest uncut diamonds in the world!*"

And they all started to laugh again . . . easily at first, then harder and harder . . . and kept it up until they thought they would never stop.